The Adventures of the
Last Wives' Club

To Vera —
Best wishes always.
Best —
J. M. Werlein

J.M. Werlein

ISBN 978-1-64416-042-8 (paperback)
ISBN 978-1-64416-043-5 (digital)

Christian Faith Publishing, Inc.
832 Park Avenue
Meadville, PA 16335
www.christianfaithpublishing.com

Printed in the United States of America

"Old age is no place for sissies" Bette Davis

Coming home to an empty house was something Marvel had not gotten used to. It had been a year since she had lost Al. Several more since he went into the "home."

She craved hustle and bustle, constant chatter, and seeing her *love* in his rumpled armchair smoking his pipe. She didn't expect to miss the aroma. Maybe she should take up smoking a pipe. She laughed at her silly notion as she set about stashing groceries. Hearing the familiar rendition of "It's a Wonderful World," she searched for her cell phone. She preferred her landline, but her children insisted she get a flip phone so she could call anywhere if needed. Simple. *Indeed*, she mused as she dug around her purse.

"Hello, this is Marvel," she answered just before the last ring.

"It's about time!" Marge bellowed. "Wait until you hear what I heard! My neighbor Vivian told me that her daughter-in-law knows a travel agent that books trips especially for seniors! I investigated it and I thought the Last Wives' Club should do it!"

"Do what?"

"A *trip*, silly!"

"Well, just what are you thinking, Miss Travel Agent?"

"I think the four of us should talk about it. So how 'bout we all gather for dinner this week?"

Marge and Marvel's friendship dated back to their college days. They met as counselors at a summer church camp. They hit it off immediately since they both enjoyed doing many outdoor activities as sailing, hiking, swimming, and building campfires. They also enjoyed spending time with their young campers and teaching Arts and Crafts, camp songs, and all the things that make for great summer memories. Marvel had always been a kind-hearted, trusting being. She knew how to have fun so people always seemed to gravitate to her. She was all of five feet one with a delicate frame; naturally wavy, thick hair; and wide, expressive gray eyes that twinkled when she smiled her large, easy grin. Marge had always thought of her as a little pixie fairy, all she lacked was the wings! Marge, on the other hand, stood at five feet eight in her prime with an athletic build. Subsequently, she towered over her friend. In her youth, she had sun-kissed golden hair, which had now transformed into white blond. It was completely straight, though somewhat thick, and she kept it shoulder-length. She had high cheekbones and a chiseled chin. Her eyes were bright blue with long lashes. She had always liked her own face. When she saw it in the mirror, she could see a bit of each of her parents looking back at her.

Their physical appearance wasn't the only way these two differed. Marvel was gregarious and never shy about talking to others, whether it was in a line at the grocery store or in an elevator. She didn't get concerned with the things life threw at her that were out of her control and viewed life generally in the big picture. Marge also was outgoing but not to the extent of her friend. She was practical, had a head for business, and was all about the details, which made her a successful small business owner. Marge preferred a plan over Marvel's spontaneity. Both ladies were loyal and honest, although Marvel had a way of tempering her honest reply's a little softer than Marge. They loved to laugh, play pranks, and, unbeknownst to most folks, could play a mean game of pool!

Even though, for a period of several years they lived in different states, they had remained close friends through letters and long-distant phone calls. Their husbands, fortunately, enjoyed one another's company as well so the two families had managed a vacation or two together at a rented cabin up north. Eventually, their families moved back to the same area in Minnesota where they had grown up. Then, ironically, their husbands both ended up in the nursing home within a year of one another. The two men suffered from Alzheimer's disease, and the women's long-term friendship took an even deeper turn. It was at the long-term care facility where they encountered Kitty and Rita. They too had husbands who had been overcome by

Alzheimer's. Kitty's husband had been the first of the four to have entered the nursing home.

Kitty was a proud woman who had ladylike manners from being raised in a prestigious family. She was a striking woman with peaches-and-cream complexion that still was evident today. Her eyes were a soft brown that communicated clearly her thoughts without uttering a word. She recalled her children referring to it as "getting mom's you-have-one-foot-over-the-line look." She had always been, what one would say, opulent at the top with a short waist, but she had lovely, long legs that she enjoyed showing off in her youth with skirts and dresses. Her hair was now a steel gray with wispy bangs but she kept it just long enough to be able to put up in a bun when she wanted it off her neck. Kitty wasn't a woman who talked on and on, like some of the women she knew. She wanted it noted when she did speak it was most often with a purpose. She was friendly but not outgoing. Jim, her husband, used to tease her about being shy, but it was truly more about her being very private in her thoughts and feelings about many things.

It was Marvel who first approached her while tending to her husband one day. She had wheeled Al right up to where Kitty and Jim were watching the colorful birds that lived in the large cage wall in the common area. After introducing herself and Al, she sat down and began to share with them about a parakeet she used to have when her children were young. Before she knew it, Kitty had a new friend.

Rita's husband had been the last of their gang to be admitted. Howie and Rita were younger than the other three couples. Rita, whose real name was Margherita, tried her best to keep her husband home as long as the doctors would allow. Eventually, his health management became too much for her to do alone. Rita's stature was on the short side, she tended to be more curved than slender, but she was physically active. She enjoyed golf and bike riding whenever she could. Rita had an appeal of everyone's happy grandma. She kept her hair short. Her eyes were a twinkly hazel set in a round cheerful face marked by a cute pug nose. Rita was outgoing and usually open to try anything at least once. She liked to stay busy and always seemed to have a project going. She had been into crocheting, beading, and quilting but only long enough that when she felt she had mastered it, she would move on to trying something new. She had been a young wife and mother. In many aspects, her friends felt she had lived a sheltered life.

These four women had been brought together by a bond that none of them could have foreseen. They supported one another as they learned it was okay to tell little white lies to keep their loved ones from getting confused and agitated due to their memories playing tricks on them. They invented new rules to old games to accommodate their menfolk's creativity when the old rules of the game were forgotten. They also made sure to make each other laugh when the pain of their journey became too great to bear alone. Therefore, they dubbed themselves the Last Wives' Club. They drew very close to one another as they navigated their way through the heartaches that their families faced as their loved ones slipped away, first through memory then finally succumbing physically.

Howie, Rita's husband, was the first to draw his last breath. His had been a very progressive form of the disease within a few short years of entering the home. Kitty, Marge, and Marvel were there with Rita and her family every step of the way. So it was as each lady watched her beloved pass on. The final goodbye was said to Al just a year ago. Marvel had known it was coming, as they all did, but somehow that didn't remove that final sting of realization that something was truly over, that her sweetheart of so many years wasn't going to look in her eyes anymore or give her his crooked smile as she tried to find ways to lighten his days. She knew, in her head, that he had no longer knew her as his wife; but in her heart, she couldn't help but believe that his heart always knew who she really was, as if the heart and brain were not connected to the same physical being. This was what kept her going all these years of doubts and what broke her heart in pieces now. She had watched her three friends say goodbye and cry, yes, but to Marvel they had seemed so strong and somehow ready to carry on in life singly. As for her, she felt completely alone for the first time in her life. Thankfully, she had Kitty, Marge, and Rita who were not going to let her fall between the cracks and become reclusive. They would lovingly make sure to pull her back into life if it was the last thing they did! So it wasn't too surprising that Marge had thought up this trip. They sounded like a gaggle of hens to others but the friends had a lot to discuss.

Marge explained to her friends what she had learned about travel for seniors. She shared that they could stay at an elder hostel, which none of them had ever heard of before. She explained that hostels were budget-friendly alternative of places to stay.

"They are all over in Europe and now throughout the U.S. You've heard of Youth Hostels, haven't you? Well, these are for the over fifty crowd. Some hostels are more like dormitories and there are others which are actual hotels. Girls, we can partake in as much or as little as we want at these places and not spend exorbitant amounts of money."

Kitty, being the most opinionated of the friends, scowled at the idea, but the others were getting into the spirit of the adventure to be had. Kitty interrupted Marge, "My college days are long gone. I have no desire to stay in a dorm, let alone sleep in a bunk bed!"

"Listen, there are also many that are actual hotels, like I told you. We don't have to do the entire trip this way but it would be a wonderful opportunity to meet new folks and save a little money that we can splurge elsewhere. Oh, Kitty, don't be such a sour puss!"

Marvel chimed in, "Honestly, Kitty, sometimes you act as though you don't like people at all!"

"Times, I don't," Kitty said with her poker face.

"I don't know about you girls," commented Rita, "but my kids are constantly on my case to get out and experience new things. I have always enjoyed trips. Howie and I would take our family on car trips, enjoying the togetherness of singing and playing games. Then after the kids moved out of the house, he and I would take mini car trips simply because we could and wanted to get away. One of our favorite road trips was to take old highway 61 all the way up to the North Shore, especially in the fall when the leaves were turning red, yellow, and orange. It was always a beautiful drive!" With a sigh, she added, "I miss those trips."

Kitty chimed in, "Well, my dear ladies, whose car should we take? How would we split up the driving? Heaven knows I will not drive anywhere from dusk to dawn!"

Marvel rolled her playful gray eyes and stated, "Goodness, Kitty, we don't even know where we want to go, let alone decide who sits behind the wheel of a car. Let's get some more details first."

"So I suggest I get a hold of my friend's daughter-in-law and get some more information about locations, prices, and transportation. Ya know, what a trip would entail!" remarked Marge.

They discussed places each had always wanted to visit. Some places were simple and stateside; others dared to venture dreams of sites across an ocean. The evening lengthened. This was going to take several meetings. After doing more research, going over travel pamphlets, and gathering several more times, it was finally decided that the Last Wives' Club would stay stateside and head to the Pacific Northwest region. They enthusiastically determined the travel would be done primarily by train. It had been a very long time since any of them had ridden a train and were encouraged by several other friends that it would be the best way to see the beauty of the country. If they went with rail passes, they could get off wherever they wanted, stay for a bit, and then get on another train to a different destination.

The adventure itself would be a first. The four of them, alone but together. Change, but a different kind. Travel can be joyous and difficult at times. Considering they were four very different person-alities, each had their own notions on how this excursion should play out. Marge and Rita were definitely the most active and stimulated by the presence of others. They also preferred plans that were tidy and predetermined. Kitty and Marvel were more whimsical, inclined to sightseeing and experiences on the fly. They wanted to make sure that it wasn't all go, go, go and to have time to meander through places, read, or do whatever each day led to. It would have to be a trip in progress, compromising here and there.

Hmmm, this could prove more out of the ordinary than we are prepared for, thought Marvel. She loved the idea of the Last Wives' Club with a hint of nostalgia and adventure. *Oh, that they could make it work.*

2

It was nine o'clock in a late spring night when the friends met at the train station. They were all very excited about this trip and giggled like young girls. They decided Amtrak was the way for them to get the most bang for their buck as well as offering travel that they had not experienced for decades. They were taking Amtrak's Superliner that had two levels. The upper level provided a full view of the territory the train was traveling through.

The train was made up of a variety of types of cars to accommodate the travelling passengers. There were several cars where one could obtain something to eat and drink. The long-distance dining car was for formal meals that were served over several different seating times throughout the day and evening. Each passenger chose the seating time that best suited their plans. One could choose an early dinner seating that began at five or sometime later up to the final seating, which began at eight thirty. The passengers were not limited to eat their meals in this formal dining atmosphere. There was also the lounge car that offered a casual eating and social atmosphere. Here you could order carryout-type food—including sandwiches, pizza, and snacks—along with soda pops and all sorts of liquor. Many of the travelers would congregate in this car to use the tables to play games.

One attraction of traveling by rail for these women was the luggage accommodations. Each could bring two suitcases for free and then check up to two more that would be stored in the baggage car. With all the opportunities that could arise as they traveled across the country, it was difficult to limit one's apparel choice. Rita, priding herself on remaining hip, was ecstatic to not be limited by the number or weight of each suitcase. As she placed each piece on the luggage cart, Kitty couldn't help but sigh and roll her eyes.

"Really, Rita? What did you do, bring your entire closet?"

Rita, being used to her friend's attitude regarding her wardrobe, just smiled and shrugged her shoulders. "I like to be prepared for whatever the occasion may call for." Marge and Marvel looked at each other in amusement.

And so our journey begins, thought Marvel.

The sleeping accommodations consisted of bedroom suites with bathroom and shower or bedrooms sharing a bathroom and shower with other passengers. The Last Wives' Club—or LWC, as they referred to themselves now—chose privacy. They reserved two bedroom suites. They flipped a coin as to who would have the top bunks. The coin toss was just a formality since it was quite obvious that only two were nimble enough to climb in and out of the top bunks. They continued to flip until those two became the top bunkers. It was soon 10:30 p.m. The ladies realized they were too wound up for sleep; so they met in the lounge car for a nightcap. Marge ordered a cup of hot cocoa and the other three decided on hot toddies.

"Doesn't this feel sort of like we are back in time?" commented Kitty. "Traveling by train, sipping cocktails in the club car, one almost expects people wearing attire from a century ago."

"It's romantic, in an adventurous kind of way," mused Marge.

Suddenly, the group was quiet as they each took reverie in their own thoughts. There was some concern, fear, excitement, loneliness—the feelings seemed to encompass and still them. Finally, Marge broke the silence and announced they should try to get some sleep so they were fresh for tomorrow's explorations.

Back in their compartment, Rita climbed into the top bunk that had been already been turned down. She unwrapped the chocolate mint left on her pillow and popped it in her mouth. She opened her novel to read a few pages while her roommate Marvel finished getting ready for bed. Meanwhile, in the other compartment, Marge carefully climbed up to the top bunk, fluffed her pillow, and laid down with a sigh.

"I believe that hot toddy is doing its trick just fine. I'm going to sleep like a baby."

Kitty, in the lower bed, was having a *heckuva* time getting her pillows where she wanted them. Finally settled, she turned off the lights.

*****

The three early risers met for breakfast, sipping hot coffee and tasting light, flakey pastries. Marvel, not a morning person, groggily joined her companions and ordered a glass of orange juice. As they sat enjoying their breakfasts, they took in the scenic view. The landscape was mostly plains with scraggly vegetation and hills off at a distance. There was a raw beauty to the land.

"Wouldn't it be fun to see a herd of wild horses or buffalo?" said Rita.

This made them all look more studiously at the scene outside their window. Once the breakfast dishes had been cleared, Kitty took out her knitting, Rita her Bedazzler that she referred to as her "gadget," and Marge began writing out the postcards she bought at the station.

Marvel, on the other hand, decided to stretch her legs and perhaps mingle a little. None of the friends were necessarily shy, but Marvel seemed to make new friends wherever she went. She had a plaque above her fireplace that her playful husband had given her so long ago, which said, "There are no strangers here, only friends we haven't met." This memory brought a sad smile to her face. Thoughts of Al made her lonely at times. Moving through the cars, Marvel took in the people and their various activities. She came across a family of five. The children, seemingly under the age of eight, were wide-eyed as they watched out the window playing a game of I spy. She approached them, saying "Oh my! My children and I used to play that game on every trip we took!" They all turned to look at her. "What a beautiful family! Your children must be *very* loved to be taken on such a wonderful trip!" She was rewarded with quick, bright smiles. Then the children's attention went back to the window.

"Please join us," the mother, Sue, said.

Soon, Marvel knew all their names, ages, what each of their favorite color was, and some of their history. It never took people long to open up to this kind, sincere woman. In fact, often after several times together, she would become Auntie Marvel, whether related by blood or not. She was a great listener and, by far, the best cheerleader anyone could know.

*****

As Kitty sat knitting, Rita began to demonstrate to Marge the secrets to creating art on clothes by bedazzling. Rita liked bright colors and bold statements. Marge listened politely and then returned to writing her postcards. Rita had taken on the task of making each of them sweatshirts that would commemorate their first journey together. She let each one pick their color for the sweatshirt and then went about figuring out what would be said and designed on each. The first one she worked on was Kitty's who had chosen a cardigan-style green sweatshirt. Rita first drew a design and a saying on a piece of paper, like a pattern. She then took chalk and began drawing on the sweatshirt, carefully planning the colors and styles of the beads she would use. Marge looked up from her writing and smiled at her friend's creativity, effort, and thoughtfulness. Kitty looked over and gently shook her head, admiring the pattern taking shape. She chuckled and nudged Marge to notice Rita's intense expression and biting her lower lip as she worked on her project. The two friends pulled out their phones to snap a picture of the moment. Working away, Rita remained totally oblivious.

The morning slipped by quickly. Soon the friends found themselves enjoying sandwiches and iced tea and anticipating their first stop, which they could take in some sights. As they ate their lunch, Marvel filled them in on the family she met. They could not help but smile as Marvel had such a way with people.

Gazing out the window, Rita jumped up and said excitedly, "LOOK! Running across the plains, they look like some sort of deer or, *ah*, something." They looked out excitedly. In the distance, effortlessly gliding along the prairie was a herd of antelope. Cameras were heard clicking away. "See! This is why I was so excited to do a trip like this!"

3

At the first stop that day, the Last Wives' Club decided to venture out, sightsee, shop, and saddle up. They headed straight to a little shop that sold Western wear, jewelry, and other knickknacks. Marvel hustled toward the hats, Kitty and Rita began perusing the jewelry, and Marge found other types of souvenirs.

As Marge looked through the Western-themed keepsakes Marvel sidled up to her with a cowgirl hat slid down her eyes. "Hey, li'l lady, anything interestin'?"

Marge laughed out loud. "Marv, you always find ways to crack me up!"

An hour later, the ladies left the shop all donning new cowgirl hats, Concho sunglasses, and some Western style jewelry. Laughing and snapping pictures of one another, they headed toward a stable that offered trail rides. Marvel and Rita were so very excited for this opportunity to see some sights from the back of a horse. Marge thought it would be something to cross off her bucket list, and Kitty was scared to death though she'd never let on. Of course the others knew of Kitty's fears but were kind enough not to reveal what they knew. Marvel had grown up riding horses whenever she could. There was a stable near her neighborhood where she would bike to whenever she had the time from chores and homework. She would help with mucking stalls, washing water buckets and filling with clean water, grooming, and other odd jobs that would win her favor to get a chance to ride. Her mom affectionately called her a "barn rat" and was thankful that her daughter preferred horses to boys for much of her youth. Rita's grandparents owned a working farm that used horses for heavy work and moving cattle. Every summer, her family would spend a month at the farm, helping with chores, learning to ride horses, and enjoying the simple life.

The women were filling out the forms for the trail ride, which asked about their experience in riding and other pertinent questions. Since Marvel and Rita had prior experience riding horses, they were given mounts with a bit of get-up-and-go. Marge and Kitty both received horses that were very patient with brand new riders. Marvel sat tall on the spotted black-and-white mare that was assigned to her. She informed her friends that these markings were called pinto and that a mare was a female horse. Rita was giddy over being given a lovely little yellow horse with a cream mane and tail, which she explained was called palomino, and that he was a gelding not a stallion. Though both geldings and stallions are male horses, geldings are castrated and cannot reproduce. Both Marge and Kitty stood nervously near their horses, stroking their necks and trying to relax. The two older geldings happily accepted the attention of the ladies. Kitty bravely tried to pet her sorrel's soft nose, and he returned the gesture by nuzzling her hand. Kitty smiled and sighed. *Perhaps this wouldn't be scary at all.*

The day was partly sunny with light clouds drifting across the sky. The temperature was in the midsixties, a perfect day to view the landscape on a trail ride. The buds were just beginning to blossom on the branches, and the air was sweet and fresh. The view stretched on the horizon as far as the eye could see from east to west.

Marge commented to her friends, "Ladies, this is—as my grandchildren would say—awesome! I am loving the feeling of this majestic animal carrying me across the land!"

"Wow, Marge! giggled Rita. "You are really getting into this experience."

"Oh, this is the way to see America," sighed Marvel, "riding horseback through the heart of the land."

Suddenly, the horses began trotting up a hill. Kitty, bouncing uncontrollably, was barely hanging on the saddle horn and begged the others to slow down. As the little band went down the trail, they could see buds forming on the trees and sprouts of tender green grass emerging from the ground. Marge and Kitty's horses, knowing they were carrying novice passengers, took full advantage of stopping to nibble the new grass or grab a branch from a bush. The ladies could try and pull their horses' heads up and kick them to go, but with fresh vegetation the horses just didn't care to obey. But if their horse friends got too far ahead, the two geldings would slowly raise their heads and do a slow jog to catch up. Their riders looking like sacks of potatoes flopping around in their saddles. Rita and Marvel could hear the giggling and huffs of the bouncing duo. That's when it was decided to put Kitty's and Marge's horses in between the others to keep them from lagging behind.

The young cowboy guide, Jimmy, pointed out many different landmarks and animal markings. They pulled up near some large rocks where the guide pointed out some large tracks in the dirt. He explained that they were looking at prints of a cougar. The group was hushed as they observed the size of the paw prints. They were assured that it wasn't still nearby since cougars cover many miles and, for the most part, would choose to avoid humans. There were plenty of antelope, rodents, rabbits, and other prey available for the predators so no need to be concerned of the cougar bothering them. Still they all looked around with caution. Jimmy quickly assessed their nerves and told them they could sing, which would warn animals ahead that the riders were coming, allowing them to scamper off. Not wanting to miss any wildlife, Marvel suggested they should take their chances but was overruled by the others. Soon they were singing "Happy Trails" and other notable Western oldies as they made their way back to the ranch.

"We really should get a video of us riding these beauties while in our snazzy attire!" giggled Rita. "Our children and grandchildren won't believe us!"

"Well, they certainly will *disown* us if they see us like this, I would think," chuckled Marge.

"Girls, never mind that!" Kitty said crossly. "I can't feel my lower body anymore. How the heck am I supposed to get off this critter?"

As Jimmy aided Kitty from the saddle, Marvel was busy snapping pictures of the various stages of Kitty's dismount. First she stood up in the stirrups then she tried to lean forward enough to get her leg over the back of the saddle and horse's rump only to have the saddle horn land in her midsection, almost knocking the wind out of her. After several awkward attempts, she found herself facedown as she swung over the horses back on her stomach. With that view, her friends were lost in a fit of laughter. Rita snorted, which made them all laugh harder. Kitty hung there swinging her legs and begging for help, which made them lose control all over again. Marvel and Marge crossed their legs and scrunched down to keep from wetting their pants. The final burst of laughter erupted when Kitty finally slid from her mount's back only to have her legs—which now felt like Jell-O—collapse underneath her and she found herself sitting on the ground. Once all were safely standing on solid ground again, the friends began their trek back toward the train station.

Slowly gaining control again, Kitty stated "I don't think that poor young cowboy ever witnessed anything like us before. I hope we didn't damage the poor kid!"

"Kitty, I have a feeling he will be having nightmares of your haphazard attempts of getting off that horse. I think he was worried you might never get off!"

Rubbing her backside, she agreed, "Me too!"

This, of course, started the chorus of laughter all over again. With plenty of fresh air, some exercise, and a good laugh, they boarded their home on the rails and decided it would be a good time to take a short nap. They went to the reserved coach where there was ample room in each seat as well as some snacks and drinks. After ordering four glasses of lemonade, Marvel and Rita watched out the window at the panoramic view for a while as Marge and Kitty closed their eyes.

The moving train maintained a constant rhythm of a lulling vibration as well as a relaxing hum. It didn't take long for all four women to be snoozing peacefully as the westbound train headed into the late afternoon.

4

Feeling revitalized after their naps, the four friends went to their rooms to change into more appropriate social outfits. Their reservation in the dining car wasn't until 7:15 p.m. so they decided to meet up in the lounge car for a glass of wine and appetizers. As they entered the lounge car, they were greeted by the family that Marvel befriended earlier. They motioned the women over.

"Please," offered the husband, Tom, "join us for a drink."

The children were all happily guzzling their Shirley Temples while Sue and Tom each had a glass of red wine in front of them. Kitty and Marvel slid in with the children while Marge and Rita sat near the parents.

Once the wine had been delivered to the table, Rita held up her glass and said, "A toast!" The kids made a funny face, wondering why they would order a piece of toast. The adults showed the kids how to hold up their glasses and explained what a toast was. Rita continued, "To the fantasy, adventure, sights, and new friends we get to experience on our journey."

"Here, here!" the group rang out.

Marvel took pictures of their new adopted vacation family and then showed them the photos from their cowgirl venture. The children giggled as they saw all the funny images of Kitty trying to get off her horse.

Marge shuffled a little uncomfortable in her seat and looked at Tom and Sue. "You two ever ridden a horse?" Before either could answer, she continued, "The actual riding didn't seem too difficult to me, but boy oh boy! No one told me I'd still feel that hard saddle on my derriere long after I was no longer on that critter!" She rubbed her backside, and the kids giggled. Marvel winked at the couple and glanced at her other companions. "How are you gals feeling after our ride?"

Kitty looked toward the heavens and sighed. "I'll need some more ibuprofen before bed and most likely another glass of wine with supper!"

Rita stood up to go to the restroom and made exaggerated bowed legs as she walked away. This made them all laugh out loud.

*****

The family left to have dinner as the women contemplated what to do with their evening after their meal. Soon they were joined by two gentlemen roughly around their ages. The men introduced themselves as Claude and Gunnar Pierson. They were brothers. Both were widowed now. Gunnar just recently burying his beloved, which is why they were on this trip. Claude, being the older brother, decided his sibling needed a change of scenery and do something he and his wife Harriet had never done.

"Well, what brings you lovely ladies together on this train trip?" Claude questioned with a twinkle forming in his eyes. Not waiting for them to reply Claude went on, "My brother and I are out for adventure, looking to try new things and redefine ourselves in our golden years."

Gunnar offered his two cents. "Ya see, my darling bride of fifty-eight years recently headed to heaven to save room for me. My bro here thought of something to stir up my life a bit would help me along to ease the pain."

"Why, that is a wise idea!" cooed Rita.

"You two certainly appear to still have plenty left in the ol' tank to have many adventures," injected Marvel.

Soon the six of them were chatting like long-lost pals. The time for being seated for dinner arrived so they all made their way to the dining car. Claude and Gunnar were also eating at the 7:15 p.m. seating. As it turned out, the brothers' table was just across the aisle from the Last Wives' Club. Dinner was served in courses. Everyone was served a salad that the LWC happily munched like hungry bunnies.

With the salads came a covered basket that contained warm cheddar garlic buns that melted in their mouths.

"*Ugh!*" groaned Marge. "These rolls will be the death of me! I've eaten two already and the main course hasn't come yet!"

As the beef Stroganoff was placed in front of the ladies, they recounted their first full day of their adventure. Each had a favorite memory. Marvel undoubtedly cherished the horse ride with all the sights. Rita and Marge had to admit that the shopping was quite fun. Then Kitty piped in, "My favorite part of the day was actually getting off that doggone horse! He was a nice horse, but next time, I'll let you ladies ride off into the sunset and I'll go find a bar!" She winked at her friends as she took a sip of wine.

There was another seating for dinner in the dining car so they didn't linger after their meal. Kitty and Marge both admitted to being quite fatigued, opting to head to their rooms and prepare for bed. Marvel and Rita had other plans. The two approached their new friends and asked if they would want to play some cards or a game in the lounge car. The brothers were delighted by the invitation. Once in the lounge car, the four found seating that was perfect to play a game, two seats facing another two with a table in between.

Marvel went to see what games were offered and grabbed a deck of cards and a cribbage board. Returning to the table with a large grin, she said, "I hope you boys play cribbage!"

"We sure do, but isn't a game just for two players?" Claude asked.

"I've played it with four players before. It's easy. We make teams," Rita told them. "We'll even split up to help you boys out."

It was decided that Rita and Gunnar would team up against Marvel and Claude. Claude kept score and Rita started the game. The competitive foursome laughed, shared stories, and played into the evening. When they all began to yawn, they decided to call it a night, but not before Marvel and Claude defeated the others three out of five games.

Giving his teammate a high five, Claude then turned and bowed to Rita. "Until next time. Perhaps we'll have to switch partners so you can experience winning, my dear lady!" He winked at Marvel and turned to leave.

Gunnar just laughed and vowed next time would be different. The women made their way back to their cabin, agreeing that sleep would be sweet after their long day.

5

Next morning, it was Marvel and Rita who were up and at 'em as the sun rose in the sky. Kitty and Marge painstakingly ambled to the table a while later. With Marvel holding a virgin Bloody Mary and Rita a mimosa, they raised their glasses to their friends' arrival. As they slid into the seats, a waiter appeared to inform them of the morning's special. Before any food was ordered, they picked an orange juice and a Bloody Mary.

Marvel held her virgin Bloody Mary out for Kitty to taste. As the waiter began to step away, she hastily added, "Will you make mine a little extra spicy please?" All of the ladies' eyebrows arched up as they looked over at their friend. "Gets the blood circulating. And let me tell you, I need circulating! My poor muscles are not sure what hit 'em yesterday. Give me a lawn chair by a pool or lake, gals. No more horse riding for me."

"Ah, Kitty!" Rita whined. "C'mon! Didn't you have a little fun?"

Kitty turned to face her then slowly smiled and said, "It was a wonderful memory, but I'm afraid what you all won't forget is the fool I made of myself!"

Marvel gaffed, "Oh, I have no doubt we each will make fools of ourselves more than once on this trip!"

The stop that most interested the ladies today was Sandpoint, Idaho. Sandpoint is a small city in the northern tip of the state surrounded by mountains and water. The friends had chosen Rail passes for this trip, which allowed them to get off and on wherever and whenever they desired. After reading up on this location, they decided to spend a couple of days here. They dressed in jeans, light sweaters, and tennis shoes as they planned on doing a lot of walking. Spring in the mountains tends to be a little chillier than the plains where they were yesterday. So grabbing their jackets, they readied themselves for the day's experience. As they hopped off the train, they were immediately enchanted with the city. They were awed by the majestic scenery that surrounded them; in fact, they stood speechless as they admired the view.

The sun was bright and the air crisp as they stopped to study a map of the city in the train station. None of them had a notion on what to do first so they flipped a coin. *Heads* for shopping and investigating the town and *tails* for them to go hiking. *Heads* won so they headed toward downtown Sandpoint. With a few scattered clouds, the sky was a beautiful bluebird blue and was bordered by the tops of mountains still covered with snow and dotted with pine forests. There was a little park not far from the station where they decided to sit and take in the view. The main downtown was three blocks long and had an old-fashioned, small-town atmosphere. Most of the buildings were rustic and quaint in appearance; many with brick store fronts. Adding to the nostalgic feel of the town were historic buildings that had housed numerous businesses through the years but now held many unique shops and art galleries. As they strolled the main street, they found some barber shops, bars, apparel and shoe stores, jewelry, mom-and-pop diners, souvenir shops, and even a Ben Franklin. Seeing what used to be considered a five-and-dime store, Marvel herded her friends toward it.

"I haven't seen one of these in years," remarked Marvel. "Remember in the good ol' days when it was a true five-and-ten-cents store?"

"I recall they always had a little lunch counter in the back where you could get a grilled cheese or burger and malt," recalled Marge.

As they walked around, they were transformed to a simpler time in their lives. Many of the bygone things that a dime store once carried they found within these walls. A candy aisle filled with taffy, Lik-M-Aid, Slo Poke, and Black Cow Suckers, candy necklaces, licorice, and many other treats that they delighted their own children with.

"Oh, look!" exclaimed Marvel. "Beemans gum! This used to be one of the only gums my Al would chew." She bought a couple of packs for old time's sake.

They heard Rita squeal with delight at the back of the store. The ladies followed her squeal and found her sitting on a stool and spinning around at the lunch counter. "Gals, they don't have a grill anymore, but they still have ice cream with a variety of flavors to choose from."

Kitty stole a glance at the clock on the wall. "Well," she said, "looks like it is ice cream time!"

Marvel knew what she wanted right away and ordered a cone with hazelnut ice cream. Marge chose one scoop of strawberry and one scoop of vanilla. Rita and Kitty were having a devil of a time trying to pick a flavor. Kitty went with pink peppermint bonbon, and Rita finally decided on one scoop of fudge swirl and one scoop plain chocolate. As they licked their cones and spun slowly around on the counter stools, they engaged the young girl serving them to tell them more about Sandpoint. She told them some places that would be good to visit, like the long beach on one side of the city, trails to hike on, a gondola ride up the mountain, and named several of her mom's favorite stores to shop at. The ladies learned that there was a ski resort nearby, several different horse ranches that offered a variety of opportunities, and many rock stores. Idaho is nicknamed the Gem State due to all the precious stones to be found there. No doubt these ladies would be doing some rock picking.

"And here I thought Idaho was only known for potatoes!" Rita stated.

With satisfied stomachs, they decided a hike would be what was needed instead of further shopping. The young girl behind the counter directed them to a location where they could pick up a shuttle that would take them to the nearby state trails for hiking. So off the LWC ventured to the Gold Hill Trail to witness Idaho scenery and hopefully catch a glimpse at some wildlife. The LWC had always been avid walkers and often went on hikes in local nature centers and around many of the beautiful lakes in Minnesota. Now to be able to walk in the mountains was an exhilarating change.

As they rode the shuttle up to Bottle Bay Road where they could hike with the most ease, they were rewarded with a growing panoramic view out their windows. The blue sky stretched across the horizon like a backdrop the mountains reaching high into the heavens all still wearing their white winter caps. There was a gentle breeze that made the jack pines wave slowly to and fro. As they exited the shuttle, they slid into their jackets as there was a distinct nip in the air. The next thing Marvel did was begin looking around under the trees.

"Marv, what on earth are you looking for?" questioned Kitty.

Marvel didn't answer right away as she somewhat crawled under some trees and returned with a long, knobby stick. "I think a walking stick is in order for this hike, don't ya think?" Marvel, very proud of her treasure, replied.

"Good idea," chorused the others as they too began ducking under some trees to find their own walking stick.

Marvel took out her camera and quickly took pictures of her silly looking companions. "Don't remain in that position too long, girls. You won't be able to get yourselves straightened up again!"

Once they were all satisfied with a stick to assist them on their hike, they started off. Not long into the hike, they heard some rustling in the underbrush of some bushes. Marvel held up her hand to quiet her friends and stop them to investigate. Marvel, ever the animal lover and adventurer, slowly crept toward the sound. With her stick, she carefully poked around. Suddenly, a garter snake slithered out from the underbrush. Kitty, Marge, and Rita ran the other way. "C'mon, it is a harmless garter snake. They eat mice and little things. No need to be afraid," she said as she bent down to pick it up.

"But it is slithery and … well, I just don't like snakes." Rita shuddered.

Marvel chuckled and turned to take the snake away from her friends.

The trail wound around some trees and came to a clearing that lead to a cliff. Down below, they could see a stream running, and some colorful dots popping up from the flowers beginning their new life. The meager grasses were still brown from the winter sleep but they could envision what it would look like in a few short weeks. It would be lovely.

Kitty was arched back, holding her hand up to keep the direct sunlight out of her eyes while she watched the treetops dance in the breeze. She too began to sway and said to no one in particular, "I can almost hear the music." Then she about fell over as she became dizzy watching the treetops swirl.

Rita, searching the horizon with her binoculars, let an unintentional gasp escape from her mouth. There in the sky were two very large birds seemingly playing in the wind drafts. Their movements were so flowing and effortless. You could see when a wind draft got under their wings as they'd soar upward then turn and come closer again. Marvel tapped Rita on the shoulder to borrow the binoculars for a turn. Removing the strap from around her neck, she handed Marvel the binoculars. Marvel held her breath as she watched, not wanting to interrupt the game she was observing. She begrudgingly handed the binoculars back so Kitty and Marge could watch the game in the sky.

"What kind of birds do you think those are?" asked Rita.

"Big brown birds," replied Marge.

"They sure were huge and looked like they could easily pick one of us right up!"

"We'll just have to do a little research. When we return to town, we went right by the library this morning. I'm guessing they are those *praying* birds."

"Oh, Marge! They are called birds of prey. You are so ridiculous sometimes," sighed Marvel.

After observing the birds' playful flight a few minutes longer, they turned and continued down the trail. The breeze seemed to play a melody through the treetops, bouncing off the sides of the mountains. The path they chose varied from spots of sunlight to the shade of the trees. It seemed the LWC was constantly taking off their jackets and putting them back on.

"I feel like I'm back in menopause," remarked Kitty.

"Oh please, never again!" came the united response.

With a small chuckle, Marvel revealed that she thought she was going insane at the height of her menopause experience. "I'm sure Al had been checking out nuthouses where he thought he would have to place me! One minute I'd be laughing, and the next I would be literally laughing and crying at the same time! I was a true Dr. Jekyll and Mr. Hyde!"

Joining in, Kitty said, "Jim would come home, go straight to the thermostat, and turn the temperature back to a comfortable number for the rest of the family because I would have set it for fifty degrees or he would find me sitting under several blankets with the thermostat set at seventy-eight degrees!"

Marge added, "My children had never heard me utter a swear word until menopause took over my being. They didn't know whether to be very afraid or laugh at me."

"My poor Howie would get so concerned because he would discover me crying at a sappy commercial. He said it wasn't fair to argue with me during that time of my life because I would get large crocodile tears in my eyes and look so distraught, he would just give in right away."

No wonder so many husbands create "man caves." There were times I would have liked to have gotten away from me too. Thank goodness for wine!"

"Don't forget chocolate!"

As they continued their hike, they took in the breathtaking sights overlooking views of the lake and city below. Overhead, they watched the treetops sway in the breeze and the clouds lazily drift through the sky. Upon hearing different bird calls and songs, they would use the binoculars to try to find the source. There were a variety of songbirds that flitted amongst the branches overhead as if investigating the humans below. The friends would be rewarded by glimpses of red, blue, black-and-white, or yellow from time to time as the feathered creatures serenaded them along the trail.

The ice cream cones had done a sufficient job of staving off hunger for a good share of the hike, but after a while they decided they could use a rest and snack. They came upon a sunny spot that had several large rocks suitable to lean against and sit on. Getting comfortable, Marge reached into her hip pack and brought out some dried fruit and nuts to munch on. Each of the women brought along a water bottle and washed the treat down with the cool water. Taking in the scenery where they rested, they decided to take some pictures of one another. Rita snapped a shot of Marvel, Kitty, and Marge posing on a large flat rock that overlooked the valley below. Then Marge quickly took a picture of Rita taking a picture and then the friends laughingly made funny faces as they posed in different silly stances.

"Girls, I'm going to have to find some bushes as I won't make it to where we meet the van without embarrassing myself." Marvel laughed.

"Well, now that you bring it up, I won't make it either! I'll play lookout while you find a good spot."

"Watch out for poison ivy and plants with thorns!" counseled Kitty. "And, Rita, no pictures of us communing with nature or I'll toss your camera over the edge."

"I would never—well, maybe I would," giggled Rita.

Having had a snack and pit stop, the ladies felt ready to resume their trek down the mountain trail. As they continued to descend, they observed how the vegetation changed and there became an increasing variety of blooms forming that would soon become flowers. Some early spring species had already bloomed, which added splashes of purple, yellow, and white to the diversity of green shades. Marvel stopped at a patch of yellow flowers and picked several, playfully inserting into her hair. Slowly, the path became more level as they approached the place where they would be picked up by the van and returned to town.

6

Marge had done her research with the help of the travel agent and found a pretty bed-and-breakfast for them to stay at in Sandpoint. Since life held no promises, the friends wanted to make the vacation the most unique and memorable as possible.

The Sweet Magnolia Inn would be where they would rest their heads tonight. The inn was only blocks from the Amtrak station so they had their bags delivered from the station. Their bags would be waiting for them when they checked in later that afternoon. There was one room with a king-size bed while the others had queen-size. Some also had an additional twin-size bed for a third person if needed. Much to the LWC's delight, each room had its own private bathroom. It had been decided prior to booking the rooms that Marvel and Rita would share the Grandiflora bedroom with the king-size bed while Kitty and Marge would each get their own room. They were registered into the Tulip and Star rooms that were located next to one another.

After their hike, they all needed to freshen up and have some downtime before figuring out what the rest of the stay in Sandpoint might entail. Kitty gladly laid down on the comfortable sleigh bed with the goose down comforter. She pulled the pretty light-blue knitted afghan over her head and closed her eyes. All she needed was a twenty-minute nap to get through the rest of the afternoon and evening. Marge hung up a few clothes that would easily wrinkle and then settled into the big comfy lounge chair to read some more chapters in the book she had brought. Kicking off her shoes, she pulled the handle on the side of the chair to bring up the foot rest and slide the chair back slightly. The sun shone warmly into her room, giving it a cozy feeling. She smiled as she opened her book.

Rita and Marvel quickly hung a few of their outfits and unpacked their toiletries so they could explore the B and B. The two wandered into the dining area where they would eat breakfast the following morning. The room was painted a light pink and had a peach-and-pink floral wallpaper up on one wall. Around the room hung pictures of different types of beautiful blooming magnolias. Small round tables and chairs made of iron and wood were placed about the room, which had a good view of the grounds. Next to the kitchen was a large table with pots of hot coffee, water for tea, and some baked goodies for the day. The next room they entered was a common living room. There was a large deep sofa with a round coffee table directly in front, several overstuffed armchairs (one with a matching ottoman), and a beautiful antique rocking chair draped with a soft lap blanket. On the coffee table were a variety of magazines of interest. On the wall adjacent to the rocking chair was a framed map of Sandpoint, Idaho. All around the room were shelves filled with books of all kinds. The room across the hallway resembled a home office as well as a sitting room. It held a stone hearth fireplace, a well refurbished wooden desk where a computer sat for the convenience of the visitors staying at the inn. There was a wicker love seat with a blue-and-white floral cushion and a wicker chair next to it with a striped blue-and-white cushion. Behind the door was a nook of shelves where board games aplenty sat neatly, waiting to be taken out and played with.

They returned to the dining room where each decided on a cup of hot tea and share a cinnamon chip scone. With refreshment in hand they went out onto the large spacious porch with several inviting chairs to lounge in. To Rita and Marvel's delight, they were not alone. There was a couple they thought must be in their fifties who were also enjoying a scone. Naturally, Marvel approached them, introducing herself and Rita. The couple told them they were Linda and Pete Jespersen from Iowa. They too traveled by train and had been in town for two days but were on their way to Portland to visit a daughter and her family the next day. Rita didn't hesitate to inquire about where they had eaten and what they recommended doing in town. She was all about having a plan.

The LWC met in the common room at five thirty that afternoon. Feeling rested and refreshed, Kitty and Marge were taken on the tour of the inn by Marvel and Rita.

"What an enchanting place," Kitty commented to no one in particular.

"Hats off to you Marge for your research and suggestion. We just might keep you as our cruise director!"

"Ah, Miss Cruise Director, my stomach is starting to awaken and could use some supper pretty soon. Any ideas?"

Marvel piped in, "Linda and Pete, who we met this afternoon, said there is a great steak place. It sounded as though they have variety on their menu. We were told the atmosphere is casual and friendly."

The gals could feel their mouths beginning to water. Who can resist a good steak? Kate at the front desk called them a taxi, and off they went for a relaxing supper. At the restaurant, the friends were seated in a roomy booth near a window that showed the glorious mountains in the distance. Soon, their server Mandy, a petite brunette coed with big green eyes and a bright smile, came to fill them in on the day's specials. Tonight, the rib eye steak with green beans and almonds, garlic mashed potatoes, and a garden or Caesar salad was the steak special. The chef's special was the apple salmon.

At this, Mandy stopped her listing and said to them conspiratorially, "If you like salmon at all, you *have* to try this! It is in a class by itself!" Then she went on to name the two soups offered, a creamy cheesy potato and homemade chicken noodle. Mandy left to give them some time to look over the menu and put in their drink order.

"Well," Kitty said, thinking out loud, "I'd love a good rib eye but it is a very large cut. Anyone want to go halves with me?"

"Me!" said Marvel. "And I'll order a side salad to go with it."

"*Hmmm!* Ladies, I'm going to have to try that salmon," said Marge. "I'll let you all taste it if you wish."

"Doggone it!" swore Rita. "It all looks so yummy, I can't make up my mind! Eeny, meeny, miny, moe ..."

But before she could decide, Mandy arrived with their drinks. As Marge took her *pinot grigio*, she placed her order for the salmon. Both Marvel and Kitty ordered a *cabernet*. As their glasses were set before them, they told Mandy how they wanted to share a meal. Then she delivered the gin and tonic to Rita. "What will you like tonight?"

"Well, when I *moe*d, I stopped on the tuna steak. Is that pretty good?"

Mandy's eyes got big, amused by the way this woman chose her meal but assured her that besides the steak, it was one of the most popular items on the menu. Turning to their waitress, Rita asked if she would take a picture of the four of them. Taking the camera, Mandy looked through the viewer to make sure she had a good shot. With that, Marvel raised her glass and toasted. "To the Last Wives' Club, may we only get better and better!"

All happily clinked glasses as the camera clicked before they each took a sip of their drink. They could smell the heavenly aroma of their meals on its way to their table. Their mouths were watering as Mandy set each plate down. Not only did the food smell wonderful, but the chef had given each plate eye appeal with varying colors and textures.

"Almost looks too pretty to eat!" remarked Marvel.

"Yes, but I can't wait to dig in myself!" Kitty answered as she cut into her perfectly cooked steak.

All tasted one another's entrees with great appreciation for each dish.

Marvel snickered, "I think we were all very hungry. We have barely spoken since the food arrived!"

Mandy returned to check on her guests and was rewarded with high praise to tell the chef. She refilled their water glasses and left them to finish their meal. When their plates were empty, Mandy came by with the dessert tray, which contained several flavors of cheesecake, a rum rice pudding, a black forest cake with cherries, and a homemade strawberry-rhubarb pie. The friends decided to share some of the delicious choices.

The sun had set, and now surrounding the silhouettes of the mountains were twinkling stars. The half-moon shone brightly off to one side and cast enough light that you could see a sparkling pond not far from the restaurant. The friends sat quietly, content in each other's company and relishing the view.

7

As the sun rose the following morning, Rita quietly slid out of bed, being careful not to disturb Marvel. Quickly, she pulled on a green-and-yellow jogging suit that she had bedazzled her name on and her sneakers. She ran a comb through her hair and brushed her teeth before sneaking out of the room. Once downstairs, she stopped for a mug of hot coffee and went out on the porch. The early morning was still a little chilly so she wrapped herself up in one of the handmade quilts that was laid on the back of a chair. She sat down on the little love seat and held her warm cup of coffee with both hands.

What a glorious morning! she thought. Oh, if only her Howie could see her now! He would be proud of how she has carried on in life, despite the lonely times, and ventured out to try new things. They married rather young. She dropped out of college her junior year to become a homemaker while Howie went to work for his family's business. She enjoyed being a homemaker and never ran out of things to fill her days, even before the children arrived. She wasn't a meticulous housekeeper but she prided herself on keeping a neat though lived-in house with cookies or bread baked each day and supper in the oven smelling divine when her husband came home each evening. What she cherished most in her married life was that Howie was proud that she was his wife and adored their children. She thought about her daughters who appreciated that she had chosen to be a homemaker but couldn't imagine doing "only that," they told her. *Only that?* She shook her head. She recognized times were different now and was thankful her daughters had more opportunities to choose from than had been offered to her at their age, but she wondered if she would still have chosen to remain home to raise and care for her family today. She thought so, but then one never knows for sure.

Allowing her mind to stroll through some memories, she recalled always sitting on the front steps waiting to hear how the first day of school went, the children around the dinner table doing their homework while she tidied up the kitchen, singing lullabies after bedtime prayers, sitting and cuddling—all day, if needed—when one of her children was home ill, and keeping the traditions she instilled in her family. She breathed a sigh of contentment.

The pleasant smells of breakfast were now wafting out to her on the porch so Rita folded up the quilt, grabbed her mug, and returned to the dining room. Sitting in a corner with windows on either side of the table, she found Kitty sipping her coffee and reading a local newspaper. Rita refilled her mug and brought back a bowl of yogurt with fresh fruit and granola to start off her breakfast. Smiling, she asked Kitty what was of interest in the paper.

"This might be fun! There is an art festival beginning today."

Rita gave her a curious look and wanted to know more about it. "I talked with Mollie, our hostess. She told me that this art festival brings in all sorts of different types of art—pottery, paintings, jewelry, and sculptures. She found many things for the inn at this annual gala!"

"I suggest that when the others decide to grace us with their presence, we present this option as an activity for today."

Rita agreed. Marge joined them soon after. The three of them were served blueberry pancakes with homemade syrup. As they sopped up the last of the syrup on their plates with the last bites of pancake, Marvel strolled up to the table and plunked down in the open chair. Kitty excitedly told them about the art festival. Marge wrinkled her nose and shook her head.

"Sorry, that just doesn't sound like my cup of tea today. You girls go ahead. I'll be fine on my own."

"Oh, c'mon!" encouraged Rita. "You like art stuff."

"It just doesn't sound appealing to me today. I'm not feeling in an artsy mood. End of story."

The ladies looked from one to the other. Finally, Marvel broke the ice. "Marge, what were you thinking you wanted to do today?"

"I don't know yet. Today, I would just enjoy a lazy day and see where it takes me." This was a bit surprising as most of the time Marge liked having a plan.

"Look," reasoned Marvel (she often had to be the peacemaker), "the festival doesn't open until ten this morning. We can just check in with one another as the day goes and see what unfolds. What d'ya say? We really didn't spend much time looking in all the stores downtown so I'm game to go into town and do some window shopping. Anyone else?"

"Sure!" agreed Marge and Rita.

Kitty decided to stay at the inn to have another cup of coffee and knit. Since there was still a chill in the air, they hurried to their rooms to grab jackets then off they headed toward Main Street. As they walked down the street, they smiled and greeted everyone. Most people responded with a smile or a hello, but it was obvious the three were tourists. They came to a little post office as they entered town and decided they should grab some stamps for all the postcards they hoped to send.

The postmistress, Lily, greeted them warmly. "Let me guess, you gals are from the Midwest, maybe Minnesota?"

"How did you know?" Rita exclaimed, her mouth wide open.

"Oh, it was an easy guess. First your friendliness and, of course, your accents."

"Accents? Us? You are teasing us!" gaffed Marvel.

"I hear it loud and clear."

"The friendliness I've heard before, but you can tell by it?" Marge asked.

"It's been my experience," noted Lily "that folks from the Midwest, especially Minnesota, have a different way of relating with others. Almost like you are sure you've met them before."

This made the friends smile. They bought their postage and thanked Lily as they left the post office. The store right next door was a small jewelry store. As they entered, a little bell rang over the door.

They were greeted by a man sitting behind what appeared to be a microscope. He was working on a necklace from what they could see.

"All the pieces of jewelry you see in my store are made by myself or my gifted wife," proudly stated Jeremy behind the microscope.

All the ladies loved jewelry, especially unique and authentic jewelry, but Marge was the jewelry buff. She had many beautiful pieces that she acquired over the years. She had long ago made sure she bought a piece of jewelry from any of their vacations, and her husband had been happy to spoil her on birthdays and anniversaries with precious pieces of various styles and sizes. Those were now her cherished treasures.

Marge held up a pair of dangling gold and red earrings. "Oh, what lovely, lovely earrings! What kind of stone are these? They are such a clear red."

"Those are garnets. You usually see the dark red stone, but there is a variety of shades that can be found around Idaho. They even come in green and other colors, though most folks don't know that. You ladies do know that you are in the Gem State, right?" The friends nodded their heads, having just learned that fact.

The store was arranged in cases of jewelry of similar colors. As the sun shone through the windows, the jewels glistened in colors of the rainbow. After admiring all the cases of the fine jewelry, Marge decided to buy the earrings she first picked up. They would add some class to a red pantsuit she owned.

Eventually, the ladies continued to look at more shops. Not far from the little jewelry store, they found a mercantile store that seemed to have a little bit of everything. There were souvenir sweatshirts and tees, baseball caps, and cowboy hats; an aisle of rock candy, giant lollipops, licorice, and gum; costume jewelry; tobacco products, and knickknacks like key chains and collectable spoons and thimbles. Rita, a spoon collector, found a cute one that depicted Idaho. Kitty had a collection of thimbles so the friends found one to give her as a gift.

Next store was a specialty wine and spirits shop. As they entered the front door, they could smell coffee brewing and something else that smelled so yummy. A gentleman with long, gray hair pulled back in a ponytail and wearing wire-rimmed glasses came from a back room, greeting them warmly. He offered them each a small glass of mulled wine as he explained that this wine, a Malbec, was made at a little country winery just outside of town. He told them that there were several exquisite wineries nearby that they should definitely visit if they had the opportunity. While sipping their mulled wine, the ladies ambled around the racks perusing carefully at the shelves with many bottles of wine to choose from. Marvel ordered several bottles to be sent to her wine-drinking daughters as gifts. Feeling relaxed after their tasty warm treat, they decided it was time to head back to the inn and check with Kitty about the rest of the day's plans.

Kitty was on the porch with who they presumed was one of the other guests. Kitty introduced her as Ida to her comrades. Ida lived in Arizona part of the time now but was originally from Sandpoint. She had her own room at the inn while she was in Idaho as she helped Mollie with the gardening and other tasks. She was a great storyteller, which she gave credit to her Indian grandmother who was of the Kootenai tribe in northern Idaho.

"I've never heard of Kootatay Indians," Marvel said.

Kitty frowned at Marvel. "It's pronounced *koo-tun-ee*."

"It is a very small tribe split by the United States-Canadian border into seven bands. There is one tribe here in Idaho, one in Montana, and the other five reside in British Columbia," Ida proudly explained. "We seven communities are the only ones who speak the Kootenai language. Although many of us live in nearby towns and work outside of the reservation, our tribal elders continue to hand down our language along with skills and traditions of our ancestors hoping that it will never die out." Ida loved to share about her ancestry so she went on excitedly, "In 1986, our tribe opened the Kootenai River Inn. We are very proud of our inn. In '96, we entered into a gaming agreement with the state so we built a casino and most recently added rooms and a spa. Due to the success of these ventures, our tribal students often go on to higher education. Some of them move on to different areas of the country, but some return after their schooling to give back to our community. Yes, we are very proud that we as a people have provided a means for our youth to become successful in different areas of life."

"That's impressive," stated Marvel.

"Oh, I'd love to visit the inn sometime!" exclaimed Kitty. "What d'ya say, girls? Shall we treat ourselves to a couple more days here and visit the river inn?"

"I just love learning things about other cultures and their traditions, don't you?" beamed Rita.

"I'm not much of a gambler," shared Marge "but heaven knows I'll be happy to visit that spa!"

So it was quickly decided that Ida would be their guide and take them to the Kootenai River Inn. Ida was thrilled to go along and continue educating her new companions.

8

Kitty and Rita still wanted to go to the art festival and beseeched Marge to join them. Marge was having none of it. Marvel chose to remain out of this discussion. Finally, Kitty and Rita had one of the attendants call them a taxi and went on without the other two. Rita was excited to get some new craft ideas, and Kitty was hoping to find a souvenir to remember their trip with. Marge inquired about the gorgeous beach they had seen when they arrived by train. Mollie told her that it was Sandpoint City Beach and was definitely a place to visit. Marvel decided to tag along.

The day promised to warm up nicely, the sun shone with very little breeze. The beach wasn't very far distance from the inn so they decided to walk. They each brought along a couple of sandwich bags from the kitchen to put any interesting rocks or other treasures they may find. After putting the sandwich bags in their fanny packs and sliding on their Concho sunglasses, they headed down the street. As they walked around, they greeted others they passed along the way. Then each turned to the other and giggled. They were indeed "Minnesota nice" and now very aware of it. They came upon a little diner just down the street from the inn and realized they were ready for a snack. The diner was lined with orange vinyl booths and a long counter with stools that spun. Next to the counter was a glass display case that slowly rotated to show the day's fresh pies and cakes. Next to that was the cash register. The friends chose a booth near the door and looked over the menus, the pancake breakfast a distant memory.

"I have to check out those desserts," Marge said as she got up from the booth. Reporting back, she told Marvel, "There's an apple crisp, a blueberry pie, a French silk pie, and a heavy devil's food cake with white frosting. I really liked the looks of the apple crisp so I'm going to go with a cup of soup and a piece of that."

Marvel agreed the desserts sounded yummy. She too chose a cup of soup but ordered the cake instead. As she was sipping coffee and enjoying their desserts, the bell rang over the door as more patrons arrived for lunch. Looking up, Marvel spied their two friends, Claude and Gunnar. "Please, come join us," she offered.

Claude slid in the booth with Marge and Gunnar with Marvel after removing their caps. Marvel told them "We are just finishing but we'd be happy to visit with you while you eat."

"Gunnar and I are just coming from a boat tour of Lake Pend Oreille. What a breathtaking area this is."

"We are on our way to the city beach to do some treasure hunting on the shore," Marge informed them.

"I am hoping we find some nice rocks. I have a tumbler at home that I'm learning to use."

"I like to find agates," said Gunnar. "Claude always laughs at my box of rocks," he added good-naturedly.

"Where are the other two banditos?" asked Claude.

"They decided to go to the art festival."

"We were planning on heading over there ourselves."

"Were you now?" Marvel said, coyly glancing at Marge with a wry smile.

As the men were ordering dessert, Marge and Marvel excused themselves and continued on their way. They entered the park under the large arch sign that read "City Beach." The city beach was made up of eighteen acres that had been donated by the Northern Pacific Railroad in 1922. It consisted of a long track of land with a picturesque white sand beach on one side. The view of the mountains reflecting in the crystal-clear lake was spectacular. As they walked on the shore toward the water, seagulls scurried away, seemingly scolding them for interrupting their day. The ladies, heads down, studied the shoreline for trinkets to bring home.

Meanwhile, Kitty and Rita took their time viewing all the art booths at the festival. They were impressed by the vast amount of creativity and talent. Kitty enthusiastically chatted with an artist who proudly made sculptures out of junk. Her works ranged from table-top-size to life-size. Kitty was enamored with one piece in particular, which the artist welded pieces of scrap metal together to become a miniature replica of downtown Sandpoint. Its total size was about the as large as a manila envelope. Rita moved on to the booth next door and was admiring the oil paintings of different nature scenes. Her favorite was a painting of a sunset over Lake Pend Oreille. The colors of this picture were so vivid and blended so beautifully. She thought how lovely this painting would look in her three-season porch that Howie built out of the kitchen. She tucked that purchase option in the back of her mind for later. The next booth displayed pictures made up of all varieties and colors of seeds. There were pictures of landscapes, animals, and birds. The friends were quite impressed.

"I don't know that I'd have the patience to do such minute, detailed work!" Kitty admitted to the artist.

They wandered from booth to booth singing their praises to each of the artists. When they reached the end of the first row of exhibitors they found a snack stand. Ordering some fresh squeezed lemonade and a hot dog, they sat down at a nearby picnic table.

"Well, well!" They heard coming up next to them. It was Gunnar and Claude.

"We ran into your comrades down by the beach a while ago. When we mentioned we were coming to the festival, they told us you two were also here," Claude shared.

"They picked a nice day to visit the beach," said Rita, "but it has been wonderful to poke around this art festival on a beautiful day as well."

"There is a lot of variety of talent displayed throughout the exhibit, that is for sure." Kitty pointed out.

"Have you found any artist that you particularly like here at the festival?" Claude asked.

The women told the brothers all about the different art they had seen and what they liked about each one. The foursome decided to work their way up the next row of booths together. After seeing all the exhibits Rita wanted to show her friends the painting she had admired. All agreed it was a remarkable scene. Still she hesitated about buying it. She decided to sleep on it, knowing the festival would still be here tomorrow. Kitty also wanted to show her friends the sculpture she had thought was special so they went back to the booth where junk became art. The miniature city replica was still there. Kitty hesitated about whether to purchase it. The friends encouraged her that this would be such a unique memento. In the end, she declined exclaiming it was still so early in their trip that she wanted to wait. Feeling weary from all the walking and standing, the four shared a taxi to the inn where the brothers dropped Kitty and Rita off. They were staying a few blocks away. They promised to call the ladies in a little while to see if they could buy the LWC dinner.

As they walked up the porch steps, Kitty turned to Rita and told her, "Be careful."

"What are you talking about, Kitty? Be careful of what?"

"Of falling for either of those two guys. Something makes me wonder."

"Oh, for goodness' sake! Men like that would never be attracted to me! They are just lonely widowers and we are a lot of fun. Of course they are drawn to us."

"Just the same, I have this troublesome feeling."

"You are such a worrywart! I certainly have never been a woman that men cross floors for so I have no need to be careful of any budding romance!" she said, laughing. Rita smiled at her friend to reassure her. She was touched by Kitty's protectiveness. Kitty, on the other hand, thought Rita, though well into maturity, was still quite naïve and gullible.

Marge and Marvel had a successful day finding shells and rocks of all shapes, sizes and colors. They had walked along the pathway throughout the park and now were ready for a nap or at least some downtime. Slowly they made their way back to the inn. They found their friends in the living room reading magazines. Kitty had chosen one of the big comfy armchairs, while Rita sat on the sofa soaking up the sun as it came through the big double-paned front window. The Last Wives' Club was excited to share the details of their day. Marvel and Marge showed off their bags of souvenirs from the beach. Kitty described some of the art they had seen, and Rita told them about

Claude and Gunnar inviting all four of them to dinner. It had been an active day for all of them so they decided to rest up for a bit and meet in an hour.

As Marvel and Rita laid down on the comfy king bed, Rita mentioned the warning that Kitty had given her about the guys. "What do you think, Marvel?"

"I think Kitty thinks of herself as the 'boss mare' and is just watching out for you."

"*Boss mare?*"

"It is the top mare who is the lead of a herd of horses. People think it's the stallion, but it's really one mare that protects the other horses and keeps social order in the herd."

"Oh? Well, I guess I should feel touched by her concern then. What do you think, Marv?"

"I think I am tired. Close your eyes for a bit, Rita." With that, she rolled on her side, ending the conversation.

9

The LWC met in the living room, all feeling a little refreshed. Claude called and invited them to join him and Gunnar for dinner at their hotel. They would meet the women in the lobby in thirty minutes. So grabbing their jackets, the LWC headed to the Best Western.

Claude and Gunnar waved at them as they entered the newly remodeled lobby. Each gentleman wore a pressed shirt (no tie) with corduroy jacket and jeans. Rita smiled as she noticed that Claude was wearing loafers with pennies in them. Her Howie had worn shoes like that and her children inserted the pennies each time he bought new loafers. As they entered the restaurant and got seated, they took in their surroundings. The hotel sat near the lake, and the restaurant had large windows that looked out on the water. They were seated by the window at a table set for six. The centerpiece was low so they could see across the table. It was made of daisies and yellow roses. You could smell the sweet fragrance of the roses all around the table.

The ladies were quite hungry as they had only eaten snacks all day. Rita was once again having a tough time deciding on what to order. Claude leaned over to her and suggested that he order for her. He knew of a specialty that this chef was known for and thought she should try it. She warily agreed. Conversation was relaxed and flowed around the table as they waited for their meals. Claude was an enchanting storyteller and never seemed to run out of stories. Gunnar was a little more reserved than his gregarious brother but joined in laughing, teasing, and interrupting a story if it had strayed a little too far from the truth. Once their meals came, conversation slowed as each admired their food. Rita looked at the plate set before her. The presentation lovely, but she was a little reluctant to dive in.

Claude, seeing her hesitation, leaned over and helped himself to a bite and smiled broadly at her. "Delicious," he assured her.

"It's elk, and this place does it perfectly. I'm sure you'll like it or I'll switch meals with you if you'd prefer"

Rita had never been an adventurous eater so trying something new made her a little uneasy. But she gamely replied, "No, no, I want to try it." She took a bite and chewed it slowly. Her eyebrows rose, and she pursed her lips. "It's very good! It's tenderer than I thought it would be. I'm so glad you had me try it."

Marge wanted to taste the elk so Rita cut off a small bite for her. Marge, in exchange, cut a piece of her trout for Rita. Soon they all were exchanging bites of their fares. All agreed the food was very tasty. As the meal wrapped up, they noticed a band setting up at one end of the restaurant. There was a cello, guitar, a keyboard, and a saxophone. The band was made up of three men and two women who they guessed all seemed to be in their thirties.

"Well, ladies, do you like to dance?"

All four nodded in agreement. It had been a long time for all of them, but they all had been fortunate enough to marry men who enjoyed ballroom dancing and weren't afraid to try other styles as well. Marvel smiled as she recalled Al boogying with kids when they had to chaperone school dances. They had been one of the "cool" parents that young people flocked to.

As the band finished setting up and tuning their instruments, the waitress came to get after-dinner drink orders. Marvel ordered her favorite, Baileys Coffee, decaf since it was late. Marge ordered a grasshopper. Claude and Gunnar both ordered brandy. Kitty and Rita decided club soda with lemon would suffice. The band had a melodic sound and played a variety of music from the forties through the present. When they began to play "Tennessee Waltz," Claude stood and asked Rita if she would like to dance. With big smiles, they walked to the dance floor. Gunnar turned to Marvel, held out his hand, and asked if she too would like to dance. She nervously glanced down but accepted his invitation.

As the four danced, Kitty turned to Marge. "What are you thinking?"

"That our friends look happy and, so far, our voyage has been fun and memorable."

"I agree. I'm so glad you suggested this trip in the first place. I think it really has been a boost for Rita and Marvel, especially. She lost a little bit of sparkle after losing Al."

"It's funny, isn't it, that we were all caretakers for so long, all the while knowing the ultimate outcome and yet somehow the end still has a way of leaving an unreplaceable void."

"I agree. With our husbands' passing, a sort of burden was lifted, but the pain is still very real."

"I'm finding that as more time passes, I miss Jim—the Jim before the illness—more and more."

"Me too! I guess when we were caring for our husbands, we just tried to deal with each day and there wasn't enough energy to dwell on memories."

"But we have survived thus far together, and we won't let Marvel navigate whatever comes alone. She had never lived alone until Al's disease."

"And then there is Rita, having married so young and Howie taking such good care of her! Do you know she never had even put gas in a car until after Howie went into the home? He did all that stuff and she did all the homemaking and looking after him and the kids."

Kitty said, chuckling, "What am I saying? You didn't learn to drive until after your kids went to college!"

"I ran out of chauffeurs and actually had access to a car!" Marge said good-naturedly.

Marvel and Gunnar returned to the table. Gunnar held the chair out for her to sit. Gunnar then turned to Kitty and Marge and asked if either would like to dance. Kitty agreed. Another oldie had them sashaying around the floor gracefully.

Marvel leaned toward Marge. "I found out that both Gunnar and Claude were on the amateur ballroom dance circuit back in the day."

"No wonder they seem to glide," remarked Marge.

The group continued into the night, taking turns dancing. Sometimes the women would just go out together to dance to a song they liked. Finally, it was time to call it a night. The gentlemen refused to let the ladies walk back to the inn so they summoned a taxi and walked their guests to the front door of the hotel. Saying their good-nights, the women climbed in the cab. Looking out the windows, they watched the moon and stars reflecting on the water as their cab proceeded to take them back to the inn. As they walked through the front door, they spied Mollie sitting in a rocking chair and reading a magazine.

She looked up and smiled as the women entered the living room. "Well, how was your evening?"

The ladies sat down, removing their shoes and rubbing their feet.

"It was a fun night. I haven't danced so much in … I don't know how long!" replied Marvel.

"Oh, Mollie! Those two gentlemen swirled us around the dance floor to all kinds of tunes. I felt like a school girl at a dance!" expressed Rita.

"And you looked like one too, Rita, the way you blushed in Claude's arms!" teased Marge.

"Oh, you! I was just flushed from all the dancing. *Um*, you don't think he thought I was blushing, do you?"

"Rita, I wouldn't be concerned. We all got a little pink in the cheeks and winded during some of those dance moves," Marvel reassured.

Mollie wanted to know all about what they ate and their conversations. They filled her in but soon were yawning and ready to turn in for a good night's sleep. They knew it wouldn't be long after their heads hit the pillows that they would be out like a light.

10

The following morning was overcast and windy. The LWC met in the dining room and discussed the day over a scrambled egg dish and English muffins with homemade jam. On each table sat a bowl of fresh fruit for the guests to eat with breakfast or take along with them. As they opened the front door to go out to town, Claude and Gunnar came up the walkway. Claude was holding something behind his back.

"Are we catching you gals at a bad time?" Gunnar asked.

"We were just going for a stroll into town and do a little shopping," commented Marvel "What are you boys up to?"

"Well, we had such a good time last night and wanted to let you know, and I have a little gift for Rita," Claude smiled. As he came toward Rita, Claude presented her with what he was hiding behind his back. Rita just gasped and couldn't say a word.

"First time I've ever seen her speechless," teased Marge.

Claude handed Rita the painting she admired at the art festival. "Oh my heavens! Girls, look at what Claude gave me!" Rita blushed as she showed her friends the gift. As Rita held it up, they all admired the painting.

"What a lovely gift!" commented Marvel.

"Well, let me put this in our room. I'll be right back"

"Would you gals be okay with us tagging along into downtown?" pressed Claude.

Kitty, feeling a little protective, frowned at the men and was about to respond when Marvel jumped in, "Why, sure. You can join us shopping." Marvel shot Kitty a stern glance.

Rita rejoined them, and the whole gang walked the couple of blocks into town. They chose to start with shops they hadn't visited yet, the first being a clothing shop. There were both men's and women's clothing. Gunnar and Claude headed to the men's section; the women were rummaging through the racks of clothing and laughing as they modeled items for each other. Marge put a long floral scarf around her head and some large sunglasses and imitated one of her longtime favorite actresses, Doris Day.

"Guess who I am?" said Marvel, getting in the game. She put on large-rimmed dark sunglasses and a bauble necklace as she hoisted up her bosom.

"Rita Hayworth," guessed Kitty, naming an actress from their younger years.

"Jane Russell," tried Rita.

Laughing, Marvel revealed, "I'm Sophia Loren! Can't you see the resemblance?"

This caused joyous giggling. The brothers could hear them back in the men's section and decided to check it out. As they approached, Rita grabbed a big floppy hat, white-rimmed sunglasses, and a chiffon scarf flowing around her shoulders. "Who am I?"

"Jackie Kennedy," came the deep reply from Claude. The women turned around in surprise. Claude and Gunnar were chuckling at them.

"Why, I am indeed! How did you know?"

"You radiate her sophisticated charm."

"Oh, you! Go on." Befuddled Rita quickly removed her costume.

The next shop was an expensive jewelry store.

"What is the most expensive piece of jewelry you've ever owned?" asked Gunnar.

"Or how about what piece or pieces of jewelry do you value the most?" added Claude.

"For me," stated Rita, "it has to be the gold chain bracelet that Howie gave me on our wedding day." She held up her arm and pulled back her sleeve so they could see it. "It's real gold, To this day, I have no idea how he managed to purchase such an expensive gift! I've only taken it off one time, the last several weeks of my final pregnancy. I got a little puffy with that one."

"I have several favorites, but they all came from my late hubby. He had impeccable taste!" shared Marge.

"That he did," replied Marvel. "He picked you, after all!"

They admired what was in the window for a moment and then continued down the sidewalk. As they crossed the street, they caught a sight of an attractive floral shop that Gunnar insisted they visit. As they entered the door, they were immediately presented with a delicate mixture of floral aroma. It was so lovely they all took a deep breath. Glancing around, they could see there was a variety of wares to look over. There were real flowers in a cooler waiting to be arranged into beautiful bouquets, terrariums that included little glass insects and animal additions, vases of all shapes and sizes, and diverse amount of household decorations. Attached to the back of the store was a greenhouse that customers could walk through. It contained hanging baskets and a variety of yard flowers and plants to choose from. As they strolled through the greenhouse, Gunnar began explaining the different flowers, which ones would appear in spring, which came up later in the season, which were hardy, and which needed tender and attentive care to thrive.

"How do you know so much about flowers?" asked Kitty.

"Gardening was a passion of my late wife's, and she insisted we tend the yard and garden together. I learned so much from her. Some of my favorite memories of her are in her garden."

"Oh, she certainly could make anything grow!" added Claude.

"Not me," chimed in Marvel. "There is absolutely no green in either of my thumbs. I even killed a cactus! How does that happen?"

"Oh, I do believe in the green thumb idea. Some people just have a natural feel for plants. I was able to learn a lot but I never got anywhere near the ability to grow flowers and other plants like my dear wife."

"I guess it's that way about most things," Kitty declared. "We all have a *gift*, if you will, with something. It might be plants, needlework, or math, but we all possess a special talent that we need to foster. That's what I used to instill in my students."

Nodding in agreement to Kitty's statement, the gang headed out the door, leaving the floral fragrance behind. Up ahead, they came across a shop that sold rocks. The storefront had a rustic appearance, much like an old cabin. Inside were all different kinds of rocks that had been polished and many made into jewelry or knickknacks. You could buy rough stones as well and learn how to polish them. There were some beautiful quartz stones that had been cut open so you could see the colorful crystal interior. They spent quite a long while looking through the store and admiring nature's handiwork. Often the outside of the rock wasn't much to look at, but many proved to be beautiful gems inside.

"When I was a young girl, there was a rock store just outside of town that my mom and I would visit from time to time," shared Marvel. "I loved going there."

"My granddaughter loves stones and is always on the hunt for agates, etc. One year, I decided to get her a stone-polishing kit for her birthday. My son-in-law still chastises me for it. It's a little noisy," Marge said with a sheepish smile.

Glancing at her watch, Marvel suggested they head back to the inn. The ladies were going to catch a taxi when Claude told them to wait. "Ladies, you should travel in style." The friends looked at one another, a bit confused. So Claude continued, "Right over there is a carriage ride. Let's see if they will take you to the Magnolia Inn."

"Oh, how fun!" Rita squealed.

The carriage was red and black with ivory leather upholstery. It was pulled by two large horses, both gray, though one was almost white. The driver sat high behind his team. Within the carriage, the passenger seats faced one another. The driver wore a red jacket with gold buttons and a black top hat. He was glad to take the gals to the inn.

Claude and Gunnar helped the ladies into the carriage. Only having room for four, the men graciously allowed the ladies the pleasure. With that, the driver, Liam, made a clucking noise that started the horses moving. Since it was a little chilly, the ladies covered their laps with the blankets provided. Marvel closed her eyes and listened to the rhythmic clip-clop of the horses' hooves on the pavement, giving her a sentimental and peaceful feeling. The town slowly passed by as the carriage made its way toward the Magnolia Inn, allowing a serene view of this rustic and attractive place. No one said a word as each took in the natural charm that surrounded them. Rita took as many photos as she could, not wanting to forget the tranquil beauty. When they reached their destination, Liam took care to help each of them out of the carriage. Rita nabbed a fellow passing by to take their picture with the carriage horses and the driver. As the ladies gathered near the horses, all squeezing close together to fit in the frame, one of the horses reached around and playfully grabbed Marge's jacket pocket with its lips. Marge, startled, jumped away just as the picture was taken.

"Did you see that? He tried to bite me!" Liam reassured her that Bonnie, the horse, was gentle and just looking for treats. "Treats? All I have in my pocket is a bran muffin I brought along for a snack later. Do horses eat muffins?"

"They love bran," he told her.

As soon as she pulled the muffin out of her pocket, both horses' ears went forward. They looked at Marge as if saying "Please?" She laughed and broke off a piece to give to each of the pleading horses. Marvel and Rita decided they had better coach the treat giving.

"Now hold your hand and fingers together flat so they can't accidently grab a finger," warned Rita.

"You need to sort of push your hand with the treat toward their noses so they can take it from your hand with their lips," added Marvel.

Marge giggled as the horses politely took the bite that she offered them, slightly slobbering on her hand. Both horses seemed to relish the flavor, licking their lips in satisfaction. Marge was drawn in by the large brown eyes looking fondly at her and hoping for another bite. She gave in, happily feeding the pair the rest of her muffin.

The ladies patted the team and thanked Liam as they walked to the front steps. Climbing the stairs to the porch, they all turned to wave at the carriage driver. Since it was still overcast and chilly, they decided to stay inside. The LWC found seats in the common living room. Rita pulled out her project, Kitty took up knitting, and Marge and Marvel picked up some magazines. Marvel chose *People* magazine, catching up on the most recent entertainment news or, more aptly, gossip. Marvel had picked up *Country Living* as she loved looking at the creative ideas and the colorful rooms depicted in the pages. As they were lost in their own undertakings, the room was quiet except for the soft clicking of knitting needles and Rita's gadget.

After a time, the quiet was broken by Rita. "*Ta-da!*" she proclaimed as she held up her finished sweatshirt.

The sweatshirt had a small flower on the lower right front pocket with Kitty's name spelled across the left breast panel. On the back of the sweatshirt was written, "The great LWC adventure" with a sketchy picture of mountains and a waterfall. Rita beamed as her friends gave the correct response of *oohs* and *ahhhs*. Kitty proudly took the garment, jammed her arms through the sleeves, and shrugged it over her shoulders. Buttoning up, she turned slowly for the others to admire.

"Do mine next!" Marvel commented.

"No, do *mine* next," Marge argued.

"Let's flip a coin," declared Kitty. "Marvel, your call."

"Tails."

Kitty took a coin from her purse and flipped it in the air. She missed catching it and it hit the floor and rolled under the claw-foot sofa. As quickly as she could, Rita was on her hands and knees, crawling under the sofa to fetch the coin. It had rolled all the way back to the wall so all that showed was Rita's bottom half. After recovering the coin, she slowly backed out. Misjudging how far she was still under, she popped up only to whack her head on the underside of the sofa. The friends stood there with mouths open but unable to make a sound as Rita lay sprawled on the floor. Marvel regained composure first and bent down to check Rita's condition. She found Rita rubbing the top of her head and laughing. Marge helped slide her out from under the sofa. Now the three were sitting on the floor and laughing with Rita still rubbing her head. Kitty took out her camera and snapped a picture.

Just at that moment, they were joined by Ida, Mollie, and Mollie's husband, Ben.

"What on earth!" declared Mollie.

Rita snorted, and the LWC continued laughing until they had tears running down their cheeks. None of them could say a word.

Kitty quickly excused herself and headed to the restroom. Trying to compose themselves, the friends each took a deep breath. Marvel was rubbing her side that now had a catch in it. Marge reached over to inspect Rita's bumped head. Ida, Ben, and Mollie continued to stand there waiting for an explanation. By the time Kitty rejoined the group, the women had settled down and were trying to recreate the story of what happened.

Ben asked the logical question, "So who won the coin toss?"

They all looked at one another and realized they had forgotten to check. Ben offered to flip the coin. With a wink, he told them it would be safer for the furniture that way.

"Tails."

Ben masterfully flipped the coin up high in the air and caught it, placing the coin on the back of his other hand to be covered by the hand that had caught it. Removing the hand covering the coin, he announced, "Tails it is, Marvel wins."

Off Rita went to their room to retrieve Marvel's pink sweatshirt to begin working on it and some ibuprofen. By the time Rita returned to the living room, Mollie left to run errands and Ben had gone out to trim a tree in the backyard. Ida sat in the rocking chair talking with the others. Just then, a new couple came through the front door. They seemed to be in their thirties, both looking physically fit, and appeared to live active lives from what they had on and carried. Both wore a backpack with water bottle attachments, hiking boots, sunglasses on their heads, and each carried a paddle. There was one duffle bag on the floor between them that looked well used. Ida excused herself as she hustled to the front desk to get the couple checked in.

On the way to showing them to their room, Ida stopped by the living room to introduce the young couple to the LWC. The ladies smiled, said hello, and politely asked them a few questions. Soon they learned that they were Stacy and Robbie Gibson from Ohio. They were celebrating their second wedding anniversary by coming here to hike and kayak. Going over each of the women's names once more, the young couple headed upstairs to get settled. Sitting back in the rocking chair, Ida shared how she envied the younger generations, mostly because of the activities they could still partake in. She had been an active woman, never marrying—by choice, she was quick to add—and tried just about everything she could think of. She had been a junior high school teacher. Teaching the youth was one of her passions. She loved how her students often surprised her with their wit, questions, and take on life. Though she missed the classroom at times now, she had a long satisfying run, and many of her students kept in touch with her. She rattled happily on of what some of them had pursued and became in their lives. One had started a successful coffee chain, others had gone into the corporate world, a couple of them had become educators, one ended up as Miss Idaho, and several others wound up in politics. Oh, she could go on and on. The ladies smiled as they listened. They could hear the love in her voice as she spoke of her past students. She inquired what each of the LWC had done in their younger days and how they had met their husbands.

Marge spoke up first. She and Jim had met in college. He had been a junior when she was a freshman. They had met at a school dance. Marge chuckled as she recounted that Jim had asked her to dance just so his buddy could ask Marge's roommate to dance. "Funny thing is," said Marge, "we ended up going steady then getting married and those two lasted about a month!" Marge had received her degree in home economics. She started out teaching in a high school but quickly decided that wasn't what she wanted to do. Jim had always been very supportive and encouraged her to spread her wings and test her talents. So she had done just that. She baked breads and cookies and sold them out of their garage for a time but they became so popular that she eventually opened a small bakery next to the post office in her town. She was only open from 7:30 a.m. to 1:00 p.m. on Mondays, Wednesdays, and Fridays so she could still be a very hands-on mom to her three children. Once her children were out of grade school, she added Saturdays as well with her children helping in different capacities.

"Oh, I wish I was a good baker," shared Ida.

"Marge is fabulous!" bragged Marvel.

"What about you?" Ida said, turning to Kitty.

"I too was a school teacher. I taught kindergarten through third grade in a public school for ten years or so and then in a private school where I also became the vice principal. It was a challenging yet very rewarding career. I too am fortunate to still have students stay in touch."

"How did you meet your husband, Kitty?" asked Ida.

"Harley and I met while bowling! There was a group of us out after work, letting off steam. I had never bowled before so my girl-friend was trying to teach me. I kept getting gutter balls so I finally took the ball in both hands, swung it between my legs, and let 'er go. It went straight and got eight of the pins while I landed on my fanny!" They all laughed as they envisioned the sight. "But I had the last laugh because this handsome army private came over to help me up. He commented to me that he was impressed with my creative bowling style then he offered to buy me a drink. Naturally, I said yes. We were together every day for two weeks before he was off to fight the war. I wrote him every other day for the next year and a half until he was finally sent home. We were married a month later." Kitty smiled at the memories.

Mollie had returned and laid out some tasty crackers, a variety of cheese, some nuts, and an assortment of fruit. She also brought out several bottles of wine. She had decided to spring wine and cheese tasting on their guests. Delighted, the guests ventured into the dining room, filled small plates with the goodies, and selected a glass of wine. The young couple had returned from unpacking and joined the gathering. Ben came in from outdoors, kissed his wife's cheek, and went to wash up and change his clothes. The grandfather clock in the corner said it was 5:00 p.m. as they all found a comfy place to sit. Robbie helped bring in a couple of chairs to the living room so they all could be together and continue their conversation.

"To continue," Ida said, looking over at Rita.

"Oh, my turn? Well, Howie and I actually met in grade school. We were often in the same classes together and hung out with the same friends. Then one day in high school, he asked me out. He had been the only boy I dated. My parents wanted me to go on in school. I tried it but it wasn't for me. Howie went from high school graduation into the family business. When I returned home, it wasn't long before we were married. I chose to be a stay-at-home wife and mother. We shared a happy comfortable life all those years together.

With that, all eyes moved to Marvel. "Al and I went to the same college. We knew each other but didn't really interact until one fateful evening. We had a very good football team that year. It was an away game at a rival school. I think the entire campus was at that game! There were several buses that took students over to the other campus, some of us drove, and, of course, the football team had their own buses. Anyway, after the game, the team buses brought the players back to our school. However, the rival school was having a dance and invited our school to join, which most of the students did. I and my friends drove back to our campus though. I don't recall why we didn't stay. So back at our campus, there were a handful of us girls and the football team. Al was one of the players. His girlfriend at the time stayed for the dance. Al and I got to talking and hit it off. Next thing I knew, we were planning to play tennis the next day. He admitted to me later that he liked that I was a bit of a tomboy, played sports, and wasn't afraid to try new things. We meant to be friends, but feelings grew and soon he broke things off with his girl for us!" Her smile grew as she told her story and her eyes sparkled with the loving memories she shared. Her feelings were contagious as they all smiled fondly at her. Al had a degree in business and went the corporate route. My degree was in sociology, which meant I had a degree that didn't provide any direction or a wide-open door to do anything. This is how I preferred to view it."

"That's Marvel, glass always half full!" chuckled Marge.

Marvel acknowledged her friend with a smile and continued, "I worked several odd jobs out of college but when we became engaged, Al nudged me to return to school. So I received my master's in family counseling."

Mollie then changed the subject. "Ida told me you ladies were planning on going to the Kootenai River Casino and Spa while you are in town."

"Yes," shared Kitty, "I'm looking forward to getting a little pampering. I'm sure I'm well overdue!"

Mollie turned to Ida and said, "Be sure to ask for Lydia and Sarah. They give the best massages."

"I'm kind of excited to just see the casino. I've never been to one," stated Marvel.

Ben turned to Rita. "Let me guess, you like to play the slot machines?"

Rita nodded her agreement. "I give myself a small amount to play with. When it's gone I'm through."

The two men went back to the table to refill their plate with snacks. Robbie chose a variety of the cheeses and crackers that he knew he would be sharing with Stacy. She always preferred to nibble off his plate. He wasn't sure why but he didn't mind as it seemed intimate in an endearing way. Sure enough, once he sat down next to her, Stacy leaned over to pick up some cheese, giving him a playful look.

The conversation was then directed at Ben and Mollie. They all wanted to know how they came to own this lovely B and B. It turned out that the couple met here many years ago as both of them took advantage of the tourist season to have summer jobs. Ben had been a busboy then a cook and Mollie had been a housekeeper as well as helping at the front desk. Eventually, they both went on to college and lost touch with one another. Once they graduated from college and returned to Sandpoint, they reconnected and fell in love. Ben worked at a local bank once he returned and Mollie was waitressing to save money to go back to school. The original family who opened the Magnolia Inn eventually decided to retire and move south. Ben and Mollie, not wanting the B and B to close or be run by others who weren't from around the area, decided to approach the family about managing it for them. The owners were thrilled that this young couple was interested in running it. So an arrangement was agreed upon. For several years, the family remained the owners as Ben and Mollie kept up the business, adding their own touches here and there. When it was apparent that no relations had any interest in maintaining the inn, the family proposed an offer Ben and Mollie couldn't refuse. They now own the inn for twenty years and had raised their children there.

The wine and cheese tied everyone's appetite over for a while, but the grandfather clock's chiming reminded them of the dinner hour. Soon they were all gathering up their belongings. Ida and Mollie began to clean up the plates and glasses. Stacy and Robbie said goodbye as they headed out to find supper.

The evening was mostly clear with some scattered wispy clouds slowly blowing by as the LWC strolled to the little diner where Marge and Marvel had eaten before. Mollie's wine and goodies sated their appetites, but they knew they would be hungry later so opted for a lite meal. As they finished off their sandwiches and salads, the waitress came and topped off their decaffeinated coffees.

With a satisfied sigh, Marvel leaned back and wiped her mouth with her napkin. "I'm glad they let us have the lunch menu even though it's well past lunchtime. That was the perfect portion!"

"I agree. Usually, I ask for a box right away. It serves me one, sometimes two more meals! Why do restaurants serve such large portions? No wonder we have a weight problem in our country."

'It's the ol' American 'bigger, better, faster' way of thinking, I guess," stated Kitty. "Who came up with that anyway?"

"And it doesn't help that most of us were raised with the clean plate rule. I caught myself, on occasion doing that to my children and would stop myself. They had to try a bite or two of whatever was served, but I never forced them to completely clean their plates."

"Me too," Rita joined in. "Instead, I tried to teach them about taking smaller amounts and quitting when they felt full instead of stuffed."

"I'm sure much of the philosophy of eating all that was on your plate came from our grandparents and parents who lived through the extremely lean times of the depression. They just wanted their children to not suffer the way they had."

"You know, as a teacher, I've always had a special interest in history, especially American history. I would bet that the rules of society and how the generations slowly transform go back to that one rule of thumb, wanting better for our children."

The women sat pondering these thoughts for a minute. Then Marge added reflectively, "I would agree, though I don't know that has always been what is best for the up and coming generations!"

"You know, some of my children's friends—and perhaps my own children—seem to expect to begin their adult lives starting with what we worked our whole lives to attain."

"I remember our first tiny apartment as a married couple. Howie and I had a full-size mattress on the floor; a wobbly kitchen table with two chairs, and a very used hand-me-down couch that I kept covered with a blanket to hide the holes!"

"Ha! Yes, our first bed was a pull-out sofa," shared Marvel.

"Nowadays, if couples don't start out with one or two flat-screen televisions, complete bedroom and living room furniture, and two cars, they think they are failures!"

"That's what I mean when I said we've pushed our generation's ideas of success on our children, and they've run with it. I have to be honest, I can't say one financial bracket has been any happier than another."

"Perhaps the reward for our length of years is, hopefully, one becomes more comfortable with who they are and can appreciate what one has had throughout life."

"Well, since we have solved the world's problems, we should get the check."

The waitress returned to see if there was room for any of the fresh baked desserts. They looked at one another and decided they had enough goodies for the day. Leaving their payment and tip on the table, they walked back.

11

The first rays of sunlight had the ladies up and preparing for a day of carefree fun and a chance to be spoiled. Ida sat idling in the inn's minivan out in the drive, waiting to take her newfound friends to her favorite respite.

Soon they were on the road. The trip would take about forty minutes to reach the Kootenai River Casino and Spa. The car was quiet with several of the passengers still waking up and the others knowing all too well not to begin chattering at those passengers if they wanted to keep them from becoming grumpy. Enjoying the tranquility, they watched out their windows and reveled in the sunlight dancing off the treetops. It was a magnificent drive and seemed to pass by in no time. As they approached the Kootenai River Inn, they were impressed how it blended with the natural area around it. The entire front portion of the inn was made of windows that looked out on an unbelievable view of the forests and mountains beyond.

Ida proudly explained that this inn recently won a very prestigious design award, "I know this award was due to the vision and dedication of the Kootenai tribe and council. A very proud achievement for my people!"

Being a tribal member, albeit distant, Ida had a specific tag on the front corner of her windshield that allowed her to park in a special spot right up front near the main entrance. The LWC slid out of the van, smoothing their slacks and hoisting their purse handles over their shoulders. Following Ida, they entered the large, welcoming lobby. To the side of the check-in counter was a stately stone fireplace. Above it hung a large mounted fish, and facing the hearth were comfy leather chairs and a sofa. Ida led the ladies through the corridor past the indoor swimming pool. Already there were families present, parents reading the morning newspaper while their children splashed in the pool.

The hallway wound around and led them to the glass-fronted spa. Walking through the doors, they could hear soft string music playing in the background and saw a large glass reception desk at the back of the room. Behind the desk were two young women, both wearing white lab coats. The bubbly one greeted them immediately. She had long blonde hair pulled back in a high ponytail with bangs curled slightly toward her bright blue eyes. Her name tag read "Margaret." Her coworker was sweet-looking with shoulder-length golden brown hair, a full mouth, and large hazel eyes. Her name tag said "Laurie."

As the women approached the desk to check in, Laurie offered them a glass of water from a cart off to the side that held two glass pitchers of water, one with lemon slices floating in it and the other with cucumber slices. Kitty and Rita declined, Marvel and Marge each had a glass with lemon, and Ida chose water with cucumber.

"Hello, Margaret," greeted Kitty. "We have appointments today."

"It's so nice you could join us today. You may call me Mags," the young woman responded. "Let me get your names and we'll get you checked in."

Kitty and Marge had both signed up for the healing body-and-sole pack, which included a tranquil tub soak, Swedish massage, and a pedicure and manicure. Rita decided on a facial and a manicure. She didn't like others touching her feet as she was far too ticklish. Marvel decided on a manicure, pedicure, and facial. Ida, leaving them in good hands, left to do her own thing and told them she would meet them for lunch.

Marvel and Rita were taken through a door that held several stations of professional manicurist and their tools of the trade. The room was painted in shades of yellow, orange, and coral with pictures of wildflowers on the walls. There was a cupboard that contained shelves of nail polish of seemingly every hue one could imagine. They were asked to choose a color for their nails. Rita chose a vivid shade of red and Marvel chose a soft pink. As they sat down at the station assigned to them, they both quickly became acquainted with the women working their magic on their hands. Happy chatter filled the room. Kitty and Marge were taken to a plush locker room where they were given soft fluffy robes and slippers for their feet. Placing their clothes, shoes, and purses in the lockers, they locked them and slipped the elastic bracelet the keys were attached around their wrists. They sat in a lavender-scented waiting area before their pampering. Marge picked up a magazine while Kitty leaned back, closed her eyes, and listened to the soothing music. Soon they were led to their respective rooms where a tub of water scented with lavender and vanilla beckoned. Here they would soak, allowing the treated water to sooth away any tension. After their baths, they would be led to another room where heated massage beds, dimmed lighting, and more of the soft, peaceful music awaited them.

As Rita sat with her red-colored nails under the ultraviolet lights to assist the drying process, Marvel moved to the chair where her toenails would become fashionable. The chair sat up on a platform with a whirlpool tub to soak feet in. Kim, her attendee, ran warm water in the tub and placed Marvel's feet in the swirling water. Then she showed Marvel some buttons to push then her chair began a revitalizing back-and-neck massage. Marvel closed her eyes and tried to make her thoughts become still. Instead, a memory of her daughter's first baby was weeks overdue appeared. Having read somewhere that often pedicures encourage labor, she took Stephanie to have her feet massaged and her toe nails painted. Her daughter was so uncomfortable, she was willing to try anything! Marvel smiled to herself. By the time the attendant was polishing her little toe, the first labor pain struck. She got Stephanie into the car and headed straight to the hospital. Coincidence? Maybe. But Marvel always took credit for enticing that grandchild into the world. As Kim smoothed and softened Marvel's feet, the massage chair stopped. She reached up and restarted the chair. Once again, Marvel closed her eyes and simply let her mind wander as she became increasingly relaxed. Rita leafed through a magazine, glancing up as Marvel's pedicure wrapped up. Soon she was drying her polished toes and fingers under the ultraviolet lights as Rita had done. Once their nails had a chance to dry, the two were taken to a separate room that contained a massage bed with lights that could be dimmed as desired. There they would receive their soothing facials. All too soon, the two women met in the lobby of the spa, feeling indulged and refreshed.

The pair decided to check out the casino. Mags directed them through a set of doors. As they moved through the hallway, they left the soft calming music behind and encountered an animated noise level, including bells and whistles. The colors also changed from soft pastels to vivid colors of slot machines and lights. Rita immediately found a slot machine she wanted to try. Inserting her quarters, she pulled the lever. After several attempts, she won a small amount and was hooked!

Marvel watched for a while but soon lost interest. Since she had never been to a casino, she decided to stroll around and see what all was there. She saw one table in the blackjack area where people were gathering and standing behind some of the players. She knew about the card game but had never seen it played. She went to investigate. She asked the young man standing next to her what was happening to draw the crowd. He responded that two of the players had been on a hot streak and were winning quite a pot. Marvel didn't really understand blackjack other than it had something to do with cards adding up to twenty-one, but she became caught up in the excitement of the crowd nevertheless. Eventually, it came time for a new dealer, and one of the winning players chose to quit while he was ahead. Marvel thought it was a good time to continue looking around the casino.

She came upon a craps table. Now here was a game she heard about but never understood and didn't want to try to understand. It certainly gets folks excited she thought. She watched as the dice was thrown but thought it too confusing so she moved on. The next area she came upon was some poker tables. Three-card poker, seven-card stud, and Texas Hold'em were being played at tables surrounding her.

Her Al had played poker. He and his buddies took turns hosting the party. The wives made yummy snacks to serve, the family said hello to the guys, and the host played bartender. But when the men settled around the table to play, the family disappeared for the in-house version of men's night out. As she watched a game in process, she recalled how Al took hosting very seriously. He always used his special navy blanket as a tablecloth, had a TV tray set up next to his chair at the table to be the bank, and usually two new decks of cards. Somehow the children caught his excitement for the evening and would beg him to let them help get things ready. Al would patiently explain what the money value was to the different colored chips. Their youngest daughter had a difficult time with the chips–money concept. Marvel still remembered how she had brought some of her daddy's money chips to the store to buy candy once and was so upset when the store told her they weren't real money.

Smiling to herself, she walked over to a table where a game of Texas Hold'em was in progress. She had heard others talk about this poker game but didn't know much about it. She knew how to play a few poker games so she watched a while, trying to figure out the rules. After a few hands, she thought she was beginning to understand the game. She had to admit, it looked like fun. Glancing at her watch, she figured she had better try to find Rita since they were due to meet the others for lunch soon.

Suddenly, there was a great commotion coming from the slots area. Lights were flashing and bells were clanging. Marvel's curiosity took over as she headed to the flashing lights. When she turned the corner, her jaw dropped and her hand came up over her mouth. There, basking in the attention, was Rita!

"Rita, did you win?" shouted Marvel.

"Sort of. My quarter did!"

"What?"

"Well, Lois here lost her last quarter, and since I had won a little, I gave her a couple of mine."

Lois was a tiny woman with short, tightly curled silver-gray hair, wire-rimmed glasses, and looked to be in her eighties. She stood speechless and dumbfound as she smiled and ran her fingers through the quarters that spilled out of her machine. When the scene quieted down, Rita gave Lois a little hug. Lois hugged her back and said in a meek voice, "I want you to have some of this as well."

"Oh no, you won!"

"Please," Lois insisted. Then she placed the four quarters that Rita had given her to play and four more in Rita's hand. Smiling, she turned and walked away. Marvel and Rita just looked at each other, mouths agape, and shrugged their shoulders.

Giggling, Rita leaned toward Marvel and said, "I don't know whether to be insulted or what? Lois won several hundred dollars!"

Marvel just gave her friend a quick hug and said, "Well, she did give you a tip."

Rita rolled her eyes good-naturedly. "C'mon, I'll buy you a stick of gum!"

Laughing, they walked off to meet the rest of their group at the restaurant. The Springs Restaurant, known for its remarkable steaks and delicious seafood, was their destination. As Rita and Marvel entered, they were greeted with an aroma that made their mouths water. They looked briefly for their friends and then saw the hostess. She showed them to a table near the window that overlooked the river. Kitty and Marge were sitting down, both looking relaxed with Ida looking her cheery self. Rita began recounting the story of her winning quarter, talking with her hands for effect and drawing attention to her bright red nails. They all laughed at the conclusion of the story as Rita showed them her eight quarters.

"Marv, what were you up to while our big winner was playing the slots?" Marvel shared about the lucky winners at the blackjack table and how she considered playing Texas Hold'em but changed her mind.

"That sounds like a fun game," Kitty responded. "We should check it out after lunch. I'd play a couple hands with you."

As they were looking at their menus, the waitress came over and quietly pointed out the window. There on the far side of the riverbank stood a moose cow with her calf. The ladies were ecstatic at seeing these large wild animals up close. None of them had ever seen a moose in the wild before. In fact, they had never seen one at all.

The waitress commented, "People refer to protective moms as bears, but let me assure you that a momma moose is just as aggressive and dangerous."

"I certainly believe that," remarked Marge.

"I wonder what animal we each would be if we were momma animals," mused Marvel.

"I have no doubt, Miss Marvel, that you would be a lioness, the queen of her pride, tender yet firm with her cubs and keeping her king happy!" Marge said, cocked of her head, and winked.

Marvel smiled and made a purring noise. "Happy king, happy home!"

"I thought it was 'Happy momma, happy family' or something like that!" quipped Rita.

"It is, but the key is making the king *think* it is all about him being happy!"

"Oh, you are a crafty one, Marvel!"

"I try." They all laughed.

The arrival of their lunches interrupted their conversation as they made room for the bowls and plates. Over their meal, Kitty and Marge shared all about their pampered morning and how they felt like royalty with all the attention. Finishing up their scrumptious meal, they asked for their check and talked over what to do next.

"Marvel and I are going to go play some poker. Anyone want to join us?"

Rita held up her quarters. "Girls, I have a date with some slot machines."

"I'll join you, Rita," said Ida.

"Marge, what are you going to do?"

"I'm going to go watch some blackjack, maybe learn how to play it a little, just so I can say I did."

Okay, then we'll meet in the main lobby by the fireplace in a couple hours so we can return to the inn at a decent time. I promised Mollie not to let you get too involved gambling," Ida smiled and said.

When they congregated in the lobby, they began to compare notes on their casino adventure. Marge indeed started to learn and play blackjack and came away with ten dollars. Ida and Rita won some at the slots so they had kept playing and eventually lost all they had won. Kitty and Marvel had also won a little so they continued to play and stopped when Kitty had broken even. Marvel lost her winnings and what she began with. They all agreed it was a fun day doing something they normally didn't do.

As they climbed into the van to head back, Ida made sure everyone had their seat belts secured. The ride home was conversation-free except for occasional comments about the scenery Ida would point out.

12

The Magnolia Inn was quiet when they returned later that afternoon. The only person present was Susie, one of the local girls who helped out during the tourist season. She was busy with a feather duster, going over the shelves of books and taking great care to reach all the crevices where dust might hide.

Ida left the ladies, wanting to take a nap before supper. They all thanked her for the fun and relaxing day. She smiled a big "you're welcome" and retreated to her room.

It was a warm afternoon so they decided to sit on the porch. As they were walking out the door, they heard the phone ring and Susie quickly answering. After a few moments, she popped out the screen door pointing to Rita. "You have a call," she said, all smiles and raising her eyebrows in a playful way.

As Rita left to take her phone call, the others smiled at one another in a knowing way and quite certain that Rita would have plans for the evening. They were comparing their colorful nails when she came back out on the porch.

"So whoever might have been calling you?" Marvel teased.

Sitting down in the rocking chair, Rita smiled shyly and admitted that Claude was the caller and invited her out for a bite to eat and a concert in the park. As girlfriends do, they excitedly squealed and went on about her date. "I can't believe it! He's so handsome and sophisticated, why on earth would he want to take me out?"

"You are a far better catch than you give yourself credit, dear Rita!" Kitty reassured her, though she was going to keep her eye on this developing situation.

*****

Arriving promptly at six thirty, Claude looked striking in his khakis, loafers, and pressed shirt, which he wore under his heavy sweater jacket with leather buttons. He glanced at his date and remarked at how fetching she looked and that he would be the envy of the evening. Rita simply blushed. He told the friends that Gunnar was doing room service tonight and watching one of his favorite old Western movies he had found on television. Holding his arm out for Rita, the couple made their way down the porch steps. As Claude held the taxi cab door for her, Rita slid inside and waved to her friends. The three looked from one to the other.

"Well, what should we be up to tonight?" questioned Kitty.

It was a lovely spring evening, the birds singing in the blossoming bushes, and a light breeze keeping the mosquitos away so the women opted for a walk. Grabbing their jackets and purses, they headed out of the inn toward the beach and the diner that they liked.

Meanwhile, Claude had found a little Italian bistro for Rita. As they walked in the arched wooden door, they were greeted by mouthwatering aromas. A hand-painted border covered the walls with vines bearing green, purple, and red grapes. There were petitions topped with baskets of green leafy plants separating the room to make several ideal seating areas. On one side were many bottles of wine shelved on a wall that ended at the bar. The atmosphere was casual, cozy, and comfortable. The host showed them to a table for two at the back corner. The table was round with a crisply pressed tablecloth, a bowl with a large floating red flower, and a wine bottle that was now being used as a candle holder. Claude held out the chair for Rita and assisted her as she pushed up to the table. Claude then sat down across from her, smiling and giving her a wink. Not knowing what to do with her hands, Rita took the fancy folded napkin and shook it out to place on her lap. She couldn't believe that she was actually a little nervous. She took a deep breath to calm down. Claude asked her if everything was al; right.

"Perfect," she heard herself respond.

Just then, their server arrived. He was a friendly and attractive guy they were told to call Will, Short for William, he explained, but he never liked William or Bill so he went by Will. Now that they knew all that, they took a look at the menus he had brought. He went over the evening specials and asked if they wanted to begin with an appetizer. Claude suggested that they order a glass of wine and wait a few minutes so they could look over the menu. They ordered a glass of red wine that Will went to fetch.

"What's your fancy, young lady?" asked Claude as he peered through his bifocals.

Rita slid on her glasses to see the menu better. She looked up and down each page. Between the wonderful smell in the air and seeing the descriptions of the food, her stomach began to growl. She giggled embarrassed, but Claude didn't seem to notice. They decided not to order an appetizer as they knew the meals would be more than enough. When Will returned with their glasses of wine, they were ready to place their orders. Rita loved eggplant but never made it for herself so she ordered the eggplant parmigiana and a salad. Claude admitted that he often made spaghetti for himself since it was simple so he wanted something different that he would not ever make for himself. He chose the chicken Milano, a pasta dish made with chicken, sun-dried tomatoes, garlic, and fresh basil. They ordered a salad to begin. Will headed to the kitchen to deliver their order and returned with a basket of warm garlic breadsticks. Claude lifted his glass to make a toast. Rita raised hers to his.

"Here's to feeling the best is yet to come!"

*****

At the diner, the friends were finishing off their meal by sharing a piece of pecan pie and deciding what to do for the remainder of the evening. Marvel decided to stay in and read. Kitty and Marge were considering a movie. As they walked back to the inn, they could see a crowd beginning to gather at the city park for the concert. They smiled at one another knowing Rita would love the venue and music. Children were playing on a nearby playground while their parents kept an eye on them. Rows of lawn chairs were set up, and one side of the stage became a sea of blankets that people brought to sit on.

Once back at the inn, Kitty and Marge looked through the paper to see what movies were playing. Marvel excused herself and went to her room. Once inside, she kicked off her shoes and decided to soak in a warm bath. She turned on the water in the porcelain claw-foot tub. She looked on the shelf on the wall and found both bath salts and bubble bath. She opened each and took a whiff. The bath salts smelled of eucalyptus and mint, whereas the bubble bath smelled like cherry blossoms. She chose the bubble bath and generously poured it in under the running water. The smell was refreshing. As bubbles began to form, some danced in the air. She smiled with satisfaction as she remembered raising her family. Her bath times were supposed to be her "alone" time. However, that rarely happened as her girls would barge in to get ready to go out or her boys would crack open the door to ask her a question. Instead of a getaway, she was a trapped audience. She smiled and let her memories float nostalgically through her mind as she waited for the tub to fill.

Kitty and Marge found a movie they both wanted to see so Mollie called them a cab. The movie theater was only a few blocks away but they'd walked enough, and Mollie told them she didn't want them walking alone in the dark after the movie. She had grown very fond of these seniors.

*****

After their scrumptious meal, Claude and Rita walked the block and a half to the park to await the start of the concert. They hadn't thought to bring anything to sit on, but a young couple offered their lawn chairs to them and then pulled out a blanket they also brought to sit on. The band was a mix of strings and horns with a keyboard joining in as well. They played a variety of big band music and more modern songs. Some of the couples would spontaneously get up and dance amongst the concertgoers. The evening was cool but pleasant. Rita was glad she remembered to bring a sweater. As they listened to the music, they witnessed the sunset reflecting off the lake. Rita felt Claude reach for her hand and gladly gave it to him. It gave her a peaceful feeling. She thought, *This is all too wonderful. I can't believe it is happening to me!*

*****

Marvel, fresh out of the relaxing bubble bath, snuggled up on the armchair in the fuzzy robe the inn provided. On her feet were soft-knit slipper socks that Kitty made. She was about to open her book then decided against it. Instead, she got up and found her pink silk pajamas. Then she slid the robe back on and went downstairs to see what goodies might be had.

Ida was in the sitting room playing solitaire and Ben was stirring the fireplace. Marvel looked for Mollie and found her just coming out of the kitchen with fresh baked cookies on a platter. She set them on the main table and returned for a pitcher of water and one of milk. Soon the fragrance of chocolate chip cookies was spreading through the rooms and tantalizing the others. Ben came first filling a mug with coffee and gobbling a cookie so he could quickly grab another. It wasn't long before Marvel gave in and joined them. Sitting at one of the tables, Mollie suggested that they play a game. Ida grabbed a deck of cards and Ben found a tablet to keep score. They decided on playing Hearts.

Marvel started them out dealing the first hand. "Three to the right," she announced.

The card game soon became the ladies versus the gent as Ben somehow continued to remain low score, which meant he was winning.

"I don't know how he does it," shrugged Mollie. "He seems to have a knack with cards no matter what we play!"

"Do you guys go to the casino much then?" asked Marvel.

"Ah, no! We agreed a long time ago that we would only go once or twice a year and make a long weekend of it with a set amount of money to splurge. Ben likes blackjack and I prefer the games that don't require quite so much concentration. I think we've been fifty-fifty with winning and losing over the years. It's just fun to do something a little different once in a while."

"You mean Ida doesn't have some sort of *in* to help you guys out?" Marvel winked at Ida.

"Heck, I don't have an *in* for myself! One would think my ancestors would smile a little more financially on one of their own," she snickered.

By 10:00 p.m., Kitty and Marge returned from the movie, bringing with them what was left of the popcorn tub they shared. The card game was winding down. Stacy and Robbie came through the front door and promptly joined them for some cookies.

"Well," said Mollie, "looks like we are all home."

"Not quite," replied Marvel. "Our Rita is not home yet from her date."

"Date?"

As if on cue, the front door opened and Rita entered. She was turning back to the front door to thank Claude one more time. All eyes were on her as she came toward them, humming a little tune.

"Well?" Marge asked.

"Oh, friends, I had a lovely time. Claude is such a gentleman. Dinner was delicious. The concert in the park was divine!"

Rita appeared to be in a world of her own. Mollie, Ben, and the others all looked at one another smiling. Crushes at any age were cute, and Rita certainly had one on Claude.

"We want to hear all the details!" coerced Mollie.

"What did you eat? What music did the concert play?"

"Never mind that!" remarked Marvel. "Did he give you a good-night kiss?"

Rita was getting flustered, and it made everyone laugh. She sat down at the table and told them all about the scrumptious Italian dinner, leaving out the detail of sitting at a cozy table in the back where they felt like the only patrons in the place. She shared about the thoughtful young couple who gave them their chairs to sit in and went on telling them about the variety of music. Rita continued, "At one point, the band played a rendition of a Sinatra song. Claude stood up and took my hand. We danced right there in the park with all those people around!" Everyone in the room was smiling at the beaming woman. "I'm sure I have never done something that spontaneous before!"

As Rita wrapped up telling of her evening, all agreed it was late and headed off to their respective rooms for a good night's sleep, but not before Robbie grabbed a few cookies to go.

13

There was not one guest who came downstairs earlier than eight the next morning. Before coming to breakfast, the LWC packed their bags. They were getting back on the train to continue west.

Mollie knew the ladies would be leaving today so she wanted to make an extra special breakfast to send them on their way. She rummaged through her recipe cards looking for one of her children's favorites. Finding it, she happily pulled it together. The guests could choose from pumpkin pancakes or a French toast, both baked with scrambled eggs, cheese, green pepper, and tomato as well as thick, crispy bacon or sausage patties and fresh fruit cups. The LWC all gathered at breakfast together. They applauded Mollie for her creation and hugged her, all feeling a little sad to say goodbye.

Ben offered to take their luggage to the station so it would be there waiting for them when they boarded the train. Ida joined Mollie and Ben to say farewell to their new friends. They all had exchanged contact information with one another and vowed to keep in touch. Ben loaded the luggage in his vehicle to deliver it to the station.

The LWC wanted to do one more walk in this gorgeous part of the country. They were rewarded by catching a glimpse of Idaho's state bird, the bright mountain bluebird. It sat (as if observing them) in a tree that would soon be blooming in white flowerets. They quickly got out their phones and cameras to take a picture. They strolled down to the city beach and park. The water glistened in the morning sunlight with soft low waves splashing on the sand. It was a tranquil scene and the women just quietly soaked it in. Their reverie was interrupted by a familiar sound, the musical call of a loon as it landed in the lake about thirty yards from them.

Marvel pointed to the bird on the water. "Well, I'll be! A friend from Minnesota! I didn't know they lived out here too."

"Maybe it's on vacation too?" suggested Rita.

They held their hands up to shield the bright sunlight so they could watch the graceful loon swim and dive. After a time, they continued their walk.

In the few days they had been in this town, more blooms were on display and green leaves emerging all around, creating a canopy of color above their heads as they walked along the park trail. They all agreed this stop on their venture became a very treasured memory. Checking her watch, Kitty informed them it was time to head to the train depot. So they turned around and with bittersweet spirits headed to catch their train. The depot was beginning to bustle as passengers arrived to catch the train. The LWC checked in and made sure their luggage was there and would be placed on the train with them. Having that confirmed, they turned to find chairs as they waited to board.

The seating at the station wasn't exactly made to be occupied for long lengths of time. There was a row of plastic bucket chairs. They found four seats together along a wall and sat down. As per the large clock on the wall above the ticket counter, they would be waiting approximately forty-five minutes. Rita pulled out her project to continue working and Marge slipped her book out of her large handbag. Kitty and Marvel were content to people watch—and there were many to watch. They noticed a young man playing a guitar in the far corner. He was playing a song that had a country tone to it. There were several people gathered nearby listening, clapping, and tossing money into his open guitar case. Next to him was a convenience store that held many of the typical travel options of magazines, books, souvenirs, and a wide variety of snacks, candy, and gum.

Kitty nudged Marvel and directed her view to a clown making balloon animals for the children and handing out notices about a coming carnival. Requesting one of the balloon dachshund dogs was none other than Claude and Gunnar! The ladies looked at one another and looked to the heavens. No doubt Rita informed Claude that they were getting back on the train today. Sure enough, the gentlemen turned and headed their way.

Seeing their approach Kitty got up and mentioned a bathroom run and stopping by the little store for some snacks. Marge put her book down and joined her. Marvel cleared her throat and leaned toward Rita. "Ah, Rita, looks like you have a suitor!"

Rita looked up just as Claude reached her and offered her the balloon dog. "Oh, I just love these things! Thank you so much."

Since there were no empty chairs by the four women, the men chose to find seating elsewhere and suggested they all meet later for a drink on board the train. The women stayed noncommittal regarding the drink offer but waved a little finger as the men found seats.

The time passed quickly, and soon the announcement was made that the train was pulling into the station and the boarding would commence shortly. Kitty and Marge returned and Marvel and Rita took their turn scooting to the restroom. With their luggage already on board, they gathered up their belongings and prepared to continue their adventure. The excitement built again as they fantasized what they would encounter on this leg of the trip.

The onboarding went smoothly, and they took their seats on the second level of the seating car to say their last goodbyes to the lovely town that hosted them these past few days. Once again, the sun was shining and the sky a clear blue with large fluffy clouds moving slowly across the sky. They could just get a glimpse of the lake with the water glistening its farewell. There was a group sigh of contentment as the train slowly pulled out of the station. Next stop for the Last Wives' Club would be Seattle, Washington.

14

The train had been traveling for a few hours as Marge finished the final pages of her book. Laying the book on her lap, she smiled with satisfaction. She loved reading about different topics from both fiction and nonfiction, which she usually took turns trading off. This one had been a mystery novel and the other one tucked in her suitcase was a book on Franklin Roosevelt's presidency. Her mood was light so she decided to find another novel to read next, but that meant she would have to wait until Seattle to get one. Marvel noticed her pal had finished her book so offered one of the books she brought. Marge gratefully accepted.

Rita had been working diligently on Marvel's pink sweatshirt and held it up for her to see before putting the finishing touches on it. Just like Kitty's sweatshirt, on the back was written "The great LWC adventure" with a mountain scene and Marvel's name printed out in sequins on the left breast. Since Marvel loved birds, Rita placed a bluebird on her pocket instead of a flower. Marvel clapped her approval.

Just then, Rita's phone rang. Rita's face lit up as she heard Claude's voice on the other end. After a brief conversation, she hung up. "Ladies, you up for a snack? Gunnar and Claude are in the lounge car and they are buying!"

Agreeing, they gathered their belongings to go meet the men. They swung by their rooms to drop off their belongings since they anticipated remaining with Gunnar and Claude until supper. After a short time, the LWC entered the lounge car looking for their friends. Claude and Gunnar were sitting at a table with several others but there were open chairs waiting for the ladies. As they sat down, Claude began the introductions. Sitting to his right was a fetching, sharply dressed man named Stan who appeared to be in his fifties holding a martini glass as he poured the freshly shaken liquid into it. He smiled at the women and nodded hello.

"Stan's traveling on business. He hates to fly," shared Gunnar.

Across the table from Stan was an older fellow who wore a white button-down collared shirt, Argyle sweater vest, and a corduroy blazer with leather elbow patches. He reminded them of a college professor. As it turned out, he was indeed one! As a professor who taught political science in Seattle, he was returning from another college where he had been a guest speaker. He told the women to call him Wally, short for Wallace. Kitty wondered how pompous he might turn out to be but thankfully kept that thought to herself. Marvel had her eye on Kitty as she knew her friend have strong opinions of other educators but soon relaxed as Kitty remained quiet—at least for now.

On the other side of Wally were a married couple who had never been to the West Coast and didn't want to drive or fly so they opted for the train. Terry was a man who seemed to know a little of everything and was sure to comment on any subject. His wife Roxanne was friendly and spoke with great volume and speed. Marvel had to wonder if either of them ever got the last word in their relationship. This made her inwardly smile.

In her marriage and family, the final word had always been Al's. It was easy for her to allow that because he always regarded her views, intuitions, and opinions before making decisions. She admitted to herself that most often, they agreed anyway. Her thoughts wandered. Al had been a fun man to journey through life with. He had been able to laugh at himself always knowing how to show his family an entertaining time. Their family trips were organized, but he never developed a bad mood when things didn't go according to plan. Enough life had happened to them all to realize one could always go to plan *B* or *C* or make one up on the fly. What did those GPS things say nowadays? Redirecting? *Ha!* She and her husband had that mastered!

"Marvel? Marvel, are you with us?"

Stirring from her reverie, she replied "Oh yes, I just was lost in some memories of Al and our family. Stan, I'm sorry I missed what you said. What kind of business do you do?"

"I am involved with imports and exports. Most of my work can be done in my home office, but sometimes the need arises for me to travel to a location where an issue has popped up."

Terry piped in with his thoughts of outsourcing work that should stay in America. Stan had often heard this diatribe shared before and was quite certain he knew all that was going to be said. He and the others politely sat listening. When it seemed that Terry was going to take a breath, Wally turned to him and began explaining the complexities of the issues. He tried to express that it was not a black-and-white situation. Roxanne, knowing how her husband could remain on his soapbox for long periods of time, decided to change the subject. Addressing the LWC, she loudly asked them about their lives, how they had become friends, and where they were traveling to. Irritated, Terry took his cue and sat back in his seat. With the others providing questions, the LWC took turns sharing how they became such close friends while spending time being with their husbands in the nursing home then supporting one another as each one buried her partner.

"Marvel's Al was the last to leave us," recalled Rita. "It was a difficult time for her. Then Marge suggested a vacation together and … well, here we are!"

"It's been good medicine," admitted Marvel.

"For all of us," Kitty articulated.

As the group continued to get acquainted, the time slipped away. Soon many of them were leaving to be seated for dinner. The LWC decided to remain in the lounge car for a causal supper. Not long after their meal, they retired to their rooms, calling it a night.

Early the next morning, the train slowed down as it entered the Seattle depot. The sky was overcast but the temperature was mild, and the forecast called for the clouds to break by midday. Seattle seemed to be the final destination for many of the passengers as they lined up in the aisles, luggage in hand, ready to depart.

As the LWC got off the train, they saw Stan standing near Gunnar and Claude surrounded by their luggage. The ladies waved hello. Claude motioned them over. They grabbed their carry-on luggage and headed over to the men. Claude greeted Rita with a warm hug and said hello to the rest of the friends. Stan politely greeted them with a nod of his head. The men and women compared notes the night before as to where they were all staying. Claude and Gunnar asked if they could call them in the next day or so to get together. Without hesitation, Rita gave an affirmative response. They inquired with Stan if he would like to meet up with all of them for dinner one night. He smiled as he accepted and said he'd look forward to the call. Gunnar hailed a cab for the ladies and helped them with their luggage. Promising to call them, the men waved goodbye.

As the cab headed to the elder hostel, the women kept watch of the city as it passed by. The taxi drove right past the fancy pro football and soccer stadium named CenturyLink Field. They all agreed it was quite impressive. The driver, Seymour, explained to his passengers that the field was used by the Seattle Seahawks, the pro football team, and the Sounders who were the pro men's soccer team. He told them that both venues were often sold out, Seattle fans were very loyal. He mentioned that if they were sports fans and had never been to a professional soccer game they should try to attend a Sounders game while they were in town. He promised that it would be a fun time. Speaking of sports, the Seattle Mariners had their big baseball stadium practically next door.

"My goodness!" stated Marge "I didn't realize these stadiums were right downtown and so close together. I always just think of Seattle as having the big fish market and being artsy."

Seymour assured them that there was much more to enjoy in Seattle. He asked them if they would like him to drive to some sights on our way to their hotel. They agreed. He drove them near the waterfront, pointing out Pike's Place (the fish market, as it was widely known), delicious restaurants, candy stores, and, of course, the many coffee shops nearby. He drove them past a live theater and right by the Space Needle, which only was a few blocks from the hotel. Pulling up in front of the AAE Seattle Loyal Inn's front door, he assisted them out of the car. Opening the trunk, he began to unload their luggage. Rita went in to see if there was a baggage cart to use. When she returned with the cart, all the suitcases were waiting on the sidewalk. Kitty and Rita placed the bags on the cart as Marvel asked Seymour all sorts of questions about his roots and his family. Marge stood by, listening with interest. Finally, Marge interrupted Marvel and reminded her that Seymour would probably like to find some more fares today. Seymour then wrote down his name and phone number, saying he would be happy to drive them anywhere while they were in town, and invited them to a café where he and a couple of friends often performed their jazz music. They were delighted with the invitation and waved goodbye as he got back in his cab to continue his day.

Pushing the cart full of luggage into the lobby, Marge went to check on their reservations. Check-in wasn't until later in the day, but the front desk clerk showed them to a room where they could securely store their bags until then. After unloading the cart, Marge went back to the desk to retrieve a map of the city that highlighted different sights of interest. The friends gathered round all peering over the colored illustrations.

"I could use some walking, ladies," requested Marvel. "My legs are feeling tight, and I'd just like to look around and get a feel of the city."

All agreed so off they went. Since it was overcast, they wisely carried their travel umbrellas. Their hotel was a few blocks from the middle of downtown so they decided to head toward the Space Needle because it seemed to have shops and parks around the area. Not ten minutes into their jaunt, they felt the occasional raindrop. Kitty put on her rain bonnet that tied under her chin, and the others opened their umbrellas. Though the morning was gray and a little wet, they thoroughly were enjoying all the cheerful flowers everywhere, the green grass, and the trees blooming in an array of colors around the city.

"I can see why some people love it here," stated Kitty.

"Yes, I didn't expect it to be so green and colorful at this time of year," remarked Marvel.

As they walked, they noticed all the different artwork displayed. Some of the sculptures seemed rather randomly placed to the women but they were impressed with the diversity of each piece. Seattle definitely was a place where the arts were highly appreciated. The LWC strolled along, glancing in storefronts, stopping to look over menus at the little eateries they came upon, and eventually choosing a little café that offered limited sandwiches, desserts, and a wide variety of flavored teas. They all gave a contented sigh as they sat down. It was good to rest for a bit.

15

Feeling recharged after their light lunch, the LWC once again began walking down the sidewalk and taking in the sights. However, it wasn't long before Marvel suggested it was time to catch a ride.

Seattle has an impressive public transportation system with plenty of buses and a light rail train. The ladies chose to catch a bus to visit Pike's Place. As they got off the bus and walked to the renowned fish market, they were struck by the dozens of beautiful flower bouquets that were being sold just inside the door. Taking out her handy camera, Rita began taking pictures of the incredible floral arrangements. Just across the hallway was a stand selling honey and honey products. Marvel went over to take a look and ended up buying some Amaretto honey to take home and a honey lollipop for each of her friends.

As they walked down the very busy market, they were surrounded by people selling handmade children's clothing, spices, wind chimes, and many unique wares. Marge and Kitty stopped at a jewelry stand where a local woman made distinctive earrings, pins, and necklaces by bending the metal and using different tools to pound designs in them. Marge picked out a pin she admired that was made of copper and silver. With Kitty's encouragement, she bought the pin, thanked the artist, and took the informational sheet. A few booths further, they met up with Marvel and Rita. They had discovered an artist who made figurines from Mount St. Helen's ash. The artist, Timothy, explained to the ladies that on May 18, 1980, the volcano known as Mount St. Helens erupted. He informed them that this was the deadliest and most destructive volcanic event in the history of the United States. It took the lives of fifty-seven people and destroyed homes, railways, and hundreds of miles of highway. He went on to explain that the figurines he created were made of the ash that spewed twelve miles into the air and eventually settled over seven different states!

"Oh my heavens!" exclaimed Rita. "I knew about the eruption, of course, but I had no idea of the extent of the devastation."

"I think it is wonderful, Timothy, that you have chosen to make beautiful creations from such a grim occasion," Marvel stated, smiling.

Rita found a mountain sheep figurine that she bought for her grandson and Marvel whose son-in-law collected eagles, found the perfect specimen to bring home for him.

The next several booths catered to spices, candles, and candies. They looked but continued down the hallway without making a purchase. They were now close enough to hear the young men selling fish. The guys would yell at patrons good-naturedly to encourage the sale of fish. They would holler back and forth and would toss fish to and from each other. The ladies had never seen such a thing and were very amused.

One gentleman approached one of the fish throwers and asked about the grouper. The young man turned and hollered at one of the guys behind the refrigerated fish counter to toss him a grouper. Next thing you know, a large fish was flying through the air and caught by the young salesman. He showed the buyer the fish and assured him it was fresh from the boat that morning. The gentleman thought maybe his wife would prefer red snapper. Back flew the fish and shortly the red snapper was caught and held out for inspection. The gathering crowd applauded as another young man began juggling several smaller fish. These fish vendors certainly were having fun on the job and drawing lots of attention to their products.

Just then, one of the fish slipped from the juggler's hands and sailed up in the air toward Rita. Rita just reacted and raised her arms to catch it. The fish missed her hands and came down at her chest. She went to grab for it and it slipped again. This time, it jumped up and hit her in the face! With both hands, she clamped down on it and pushed it into her cheek. Those around her were speechless and a bit stunned. The young juggler looked horrified. Marge and Marvel were briefly astonished burst out laughing. Kitty joined in too, slapping her thigh.

Rita took the fish, looked at it, and commented, "Well, hello! Thanks for dropping in!" Then she too was lost in fits of giggles followed soon with snorting.

Relieved, the young juggler smiled shyly and shrugged his shoulders. His buddies were not going to let him live this one down! Handing the fish back to the juggler, she looked at her hands and asked if they had a sink where she could wash the fishy smell off her hands and face. He put the fish on the back counter and pointed Rita in the direction of the lady's restroom.

After that hardy bout of laughter, they all decided to pay a visit to the lady's room, so they fell in behind Rita. While washing up in the restroom, a young woman approached Rita holding up her phone to show her a picture of Rita holding the fish in front of her face and talking to it. Her expression was priceless. Her eyebrows were raised, eyes wide, and mouth curved in an *O* shape. Rita's cheeks quickly turned a bright pink as her friends peered over her shoulder seeing the photo.

Laughing, Marge held her hands up to the side of her face, palms facing backward, and swung them open and closed as she pursed her lips and said, "Ladies, shall we swim on?"

Rita gave the young gal her phone number so she could send the picture to her. Thanking her, she hustled out behind her pals.

Several booths from the restroom, they came upon an assortment of fruits. There were Washington apples cut into pieces along with samples of oranges and strawberries available to taste. The LWC happily tried all varieties, discussing the tartness or sweetness of each sample. Before moving on, they bought several apples and oranges to take back to their rooms. Kitty gave a large yawn and declared it was her naptime. The yawning, being contagious, prompted them to catch a bus back to their hostel but not before they stopped to buy a couple bouquets of the colorful flowers that they passed on their way.

Arriving at the elder hostel, they were relieved to find out their rooms were ready so they could take their luggage and unpack before lying down. Their rooms were all in the same hallway, three of them on one side of the hall and one straight across. Marge, "driving" the baggage cart, had trouble getting it straight out of the elevator door, banging it several times on the corner, and swearing to herself. Marvel took the other side only to have her bag of fruit slide out of her hands, spilling apples and oranges across the carpet. Rita began to crouch down to help pick them up, but Kitty stopped her. "No, Rita! Remember the last time you tried to retrieve a fallen object and you banged your head?"

Marvel kneeled down to reload her fruit into the bag when Marge managed to straighten the cart and pushed it, running over Marvel's foot. "*Ouch!* Marge, what the heck are you doing?"

"I'm sorry, but I suddenly got this thing working. Are you okay?"

"Other than missing three toes, I'm fine!" Marvel moaned.

"What?"

"I'm kidding about the toes, but that really hurt!"

Kitty handed her bags to Rita and leaned over to assist Marvel back to a vertical position. "Marv, can you stand on it?"

"Yes, yes, it's only bruised, I think." Being upright again, she handed her bag of fruit to Kitty and grasped the other side of the cart. "Careful, Marge. I would appreciate you not running over my other foot!"

The two successfully moved the cart in front of their rooms without damaging the walls or more toes. Rita had gone ahead to unlock her door, put down the packages, and grab a bucket to get some ice for Marvel's foot.

Once the cart was unloaded, Marvel sat on her bed with the pillows propped up behind her and her foot elevated with towels as Rita placed the bag of ice on her foot. "*Uff da!* That is cold! Can't we wrap it in something?"

Marge brought a towel from her room to wrap the bag of ice along with some ibuprofen. She apologized for the fifth time as she looked at her friend's black and blue foot. She placed a sweater coat around Marvel's shoulders and up under her chin to keep her warm. Marvel closed her eyes and told her caregivers to go take a nap as she intended to do the same. They left quietly and shut the door.

16

Marvel was dreaming of playing on the swing set at the play-ground with her granddaughters, just getting ready to leap from the swing when a persistent knock on her door awakened her. Slowly her head cleared, and she responded. "Come in!"

"I can't, the door is locked."

"Coming, coming!" Sliding off the bed and gingerly setting her bruised foot down, she attempted to stand. Though her foot throbbed, she could put weight on it and hobble over to the door. Opening it, she found Rita looking embarrassed.

"Sorry, Marv. We should have opened the bolt in your door so the door couldn't close all the way and lock. Did I wake you?"

"I slept long enough. What's up?"

Well, Claude called, and he and Gunnar were wondering if we would like to 'double date' tonight. They would treat us to a seafood dinner."

"I really am not in the mood to be social tonight Rita. Sorry. Can't you ask one of the others?"

"Kitty is suspicious of them, and … well, he asked specifically for you."

"Sorry, I think not." Marvel pointed down to her colorful foot and made her way over to the side of the bed to sit.

Rita sighed, "Oh, how could I forget? You poor thing! I guess I don't think very clearly after I talk with Claude. He is so charming and sweet. I love the little twang in his voice. Wonder if he ever lived in Texas? I'll have to ask him."

Marvel shut her eyes momentarily and slightly shook her head. It seemed her friend was getting swooned. "Regardless, I can't help you out tonight. You'll have to ask Marge."

Disappointedly, Rita gave Marvel a quick hug and left to head to Marge's room. On the way, she started practicing what she would say to convince her friend to be the final wheel of a foursome. But Marge wasn't in her room. Rita found her in Kitty's. The two were eating an orange. Rita took a deep breath and hoped Kitty wouldn't say anything about the boys. Helping herself to a wedge of the juicy orange, Rita inquired about any plans for the evening, telling them that Marvel wasn't in the mood to do much.

"We were just talking about that," said Marge "Any ideas?"

"Well, you see ... *um*, I was thinking ... well, actually, I was going to see—"

"Spit it out! I'm guessing you want to include your 'boyfriend'," Kitty quipped. She had minimal tolerance for beating around the bush.

"Actually, I was seeing if Marge would like to, sort of—casually, of course—"

"What?"

"Double date with Claude and me tonight. He and Gunnar would like to treat us to a seafood dinner."

Marge looked a little confused at Rita and then glanced over at Kitty. "We figured Gunnar had a soft spot for Marvel."

"Okay, he did ask about Marvel, but she's not up to it and I think it would be fun!"

Marge was silent, pondering the invitation.

"Oh, for heaven's sake, just go!" prodded Kitty. Then she winked at Rita.

With raised hopes, Rita gave Marge her most pleading expression. Marge laughed. "Okay, okay. But if that ol' coot tries to hold my hand or give me a goodnight kiss, I'll not have it. He will encounter my knuckle." Demonstrating what she meant, she closed her fist with the middle finger's knuckle raised higher than the others to provide a little more *oomph* on impact.

"Thank you! Thank you! It will be fun, you'll see!"

With Marge and Rita's evening planned, Kitty went to visit Marvel and see if she could bring her anything. Perhaps they could have a picnic in the room and watch a movie together. Marvel's door was ajar so Kitty knocked once and entered. Marvel was back sitting on her bed with her foot elevated. Kitty slid onto the other end of the bed to face her friend and suggested her plan for the evening. It sounded perfect. Marvel set about checking on movies they would be interested in watching and Kitty called the front desk to inquire about nearby markets or restaurants where she could pick up some takeout.

Before heading downstairs to wait for their dates, Marge and Rita stopped in to check on Marvel. Marge wore a nice pair of khaki pants and a purple sweater set with a simple pearl necklace strand and dropped earrings. Rita donned her red blouse that tied in a large draping bow at the neck, gray slacks, and a white sweater across her shoulders with a sliver chain connecting the two open sides. In her hair, she wore a gardenia that was pinned with a rhinestone bobby pin. They both looked like they were ready for a night on the town. Marvel heartily gave them her approval. Glowing Rita led the way to the elevator. Kitty was stepping off as the two were about to get on. She was carrying a couple of bags that had delicious smells pouring from them. Wishing them a fun evening, she headed to Marvel's room to set out the picnic.

Kitty had found a local market that had a deli with much to choose from. Being in Washington, it also sold alcohol so she grabbed a bottle of wine. She had bought some grilled chicken, potato salad, fresh fruit salad, and brownies for dessert. She laid out a towel on the bed and placed the food before them. In a separate bag were plates, plastic utensils, and napkins. Marvel dug in her purse and produced a corkscrew wine opener and proceeded to open the bottle of *cabernet*. After pouring it into their plastic glasses, they touched rims and toasted friendship. While waiting downstairs Rita kept glancing in the mirror and fussing with her hair, sweater, and makeup. Finally, Marge told her to stop or she would slap her hand.

Getting out of a waiting cab, Claude came forward to escort them. Claude immediately praised how lovely they both looked and commented to Rita how much he liked the flower in her hair. Rita's cheeks turned pink. He explained that Gunnar was already at the restaurant securing a good table. Claude opened the rear door, Rita slipped into the middle, and Marge sliding next to her. Claude went around and got in the other door. After buckling their seat belts, the taxi driver pulled out from his parking spot and headed to the restaurant.

17

The picnic back at the room was the right choice for a relaxed evening. Kitty and Marvel nibbled on the food and sipped their wine as they watched an old Cary Grant and Kathrine Hepburn movie. Marvel yawned and quickly apologized to Kitty. She didn't want her friend to think she was bored. She was a little surprised how much energy getting injured had taken out of her. Her foot looked like a painting with all the many shades of blue and purple. At least the ice had kept any swelling down to a minimum, and she was thankful for that.

During a commercial, Kitty, often blunt and not hiding her distrust, asked Marvel what she thought of the *boys*, as she called Claude and Gunnar.

Knowing her friend, Marvel knew this question would be coming sooner or later. She looked directly at Kitty and stated, "I guess I don't think much of anything about them. They are kind of fun, polite, and easy to be around. Why? Don't you like them?"

"It's not that I don't like them. They just come on too strong and too, too smooth."

"They are lonely. And let's face it, we are lots of fun, smart, and admirable women! Besides, men just need female companionship to round off their lives!"

"That goes to show you."

"Show me what?"

"That God had to create women because men need nurturing, wisdom, and guidance in life, and they can't live without us. Now we, on the other hand, do quite nicely with or without men. Don't get me wrong, there are men I've been quite fond of over the years, but I am happy and content alone too! What is that verse in that Mary

Poppins song? 'Though we adore men individually, we agree that as a group they're rather stupid'."

"Oh, Kitty! You can be just awful!" Marvel laughed.

"*Haha*! To us! Cheers!"

Sipping their wine, they turned their attention to the returning movie.

*****

The brothers had a very special venue in mind to treat the ladies for dinner. As the cab pulled up to the waterfront restaurant, Rita read the sign out loud. "Elliot's Oyster House. I can honestly say that I have never eaten oyster. Is that all they serve?" Realizing how ungrateful that sounded she quickly tried to cover her tracks. "I mean—Oh dear! I didn't mean to insult you, boys. I'm just concerned that I might not like oyster. Oh, I'm sorry. I should have kept my mouth shut!"

Claude leaned over to her and gently said, "Please don't worry, no insult was taken. And yes, other things are served here. They just happen to be known for the freshest oysters in Seattle. Gunnar and I will order some for an appetizer and you can try it or not. I know oysters are not everyone's cup of tea but, Rita, don't forget you liked the elk I encouraged you to try." Winking, he squeezed her arm.

Marge added, "I have never tried oysters either, Rita. Let's go out on a limb and give it a whirl. Nothing ventured nothing gained, right?"

Rita whispered in Marge's ear, "But I'm worried I won't like the texture and gag. I would be so embarrassed!"

Marge smiled at her friend and said, "I'll go first."

As the threesome approached the hostess, she motioned to the back corner of the restaurant to a table right on the water. There sat Gunnar dressed in cowboy boots, jeans, and chambray shirt with a corduroy jacket. Around his neck hung a bolo tie with a large turquoise stone. He saw them and waved enthusiastically. He stood as they approached. The men held out a chair for the ladies to sit, making sure the women had full view of the water. They helped them push in their chairs before taking their seats.

The waitress, Daphne, came to take their drink orders. Gunnar was already nursing his Scotch and soda. Claude ordered some white wine for himself and their companions. With their drinks taken care of, they turned their attention to the menu. Claude relayed the conversation regarding oysters to Gunnar, and they decided to choose the mildest of the oysters for their appetizers. The brothers loved all kinds of foods and were happy to be adventurist, therefore they had developed a taste for the mollusks long ago but were very aware many others didn't share that appreciation. When Daphne returned with their drinks, Gunnar told her that they would like an order of the South Sound Kumamoto found in South Puget Sound right there in Washington. Continuing to peruse the menu, they discussed the different options. Marge said she loved salmon, and being from the Midwest, it was usually a long trip to the supermarket or local restaurants. She chose the Alaskan coho salmon. Gunnar pointed to the roasted lobster tail. Daphne nodded. Now she turned to Rita and Claude. "What can I get for you two?"

Rita started to order the grilled seafood salad, but Claude interrupted and told her that he would be most pleased if she chose something a little more special. Marge had to admit Claude read Rita well. She didn't want him spending too much money on her. Rita looked at him and shrugged her shoulders.

"I'll order first," he commented. Claude also ordered the lobster tail.

Now it was Rita's turn to pick what she wanted to order. She *ummed* and *ahhed* but finally decided on the steamed Dungeness crab. They noticed that their waitress didn't write down any of their orders and wondered how she could keep it all straight in her head. They were impressed. It wasn't long after Daphne took their order that she returned with the oysters. Both Marge and Rita couldn't help but stare at the slimy meat tucked inside the half shell. Gunnar and Claude happily picked up a shell and toasted one another, touched shells, and then tipped the meat down their throats. Rita could feel the bile rise in her throat. She should confess right now that she didn't want to be brave and try yet another new entrée. Yes, the elk had been tasty and she would even order that again, but this? The boys encouraged Marge and Rita to try. Marge daringly took one and put some sauce on it as she had seen the boys do. She lifted the shell and opened her mouth. There was one problem. Instead of the slimy portion sliding down her throat, it stuck in the back of her mouth. She found herself chewing and couldn't take it another moment. She grabbed her napkin and spit the meat out. Coughing, she apologized but claimed she couldn't go through with it. That was the out Rita needed.

"Boys, I'm sorry, but I know if Marge couldn't handle it, there is no way I could. I can't even do a shot. It seems to me that is not how you are supposed to eat oysters!" She glanced at Marge who was gulping her water, nodding her head.

The brothers smiled and comforted the women. "No problem, ladies. Not all foods are for everyone."

"Marge, I'm impressed you got as far as you did," commented Gunnar. He admired her spunk. He began to think he would like to know more about her.

Gratefully, they turned their attention to their drinks and bread that had been provided. By the time the boys finished off the oysters, Daphne appeared with their main dishes.

"Oh my heavens, smell that scrumptious salmon!"

"I'm busy admiring my succulent crab!"

As Daphne took away the empty oyster dish and glasses, she inquired if there was anything else they wanted. Both Claude and Gunnar requested refills of their beverages. The girls assured the waitress they were fine for the moment. The conversation stalled as each enjoyed their meal. After a few bites Claude asked the others about their food. All agreed it was delicious. Pretty soon they were tasting one another's entrée.

Rita looked out to the pier that surrounded them and pointed her finger. All she could do was point her finger and say, "Look!" As the sun was sinking on the horizon, they could make out a pod of dolphins jumping and playing in the water. "They look like they are having so much fun, don't they?"

"Have you girls ever seen a dolphin up close?" Gunnar asked.

"No, but I would love to! My daughter's family went swimming with dolphins when they went on a Caribbean vacation once,"

Marge shared. Wouldn't that be amazing? Now that is something I would get in the ocean for!"

"Marge, you don't like water!"

"Oh, I love the water and I still swim, but I have never been keen on swimming in the ocean. I probably have seen too many nature shows. I'm a little too leery of what lies underneath the surface that I cannot see. What about you, boys? Ever been close to dolphins?"

"No, but I sure would like the chance to swim with them sometime. Maybe on our next trip, eh, Gunnar?"

Just then, a large seagull flew up to the railing that was outside of their window. In its mouth was a small fish that it tossed up into the air to swallow it lengthwise. Afterward, it peered in the window seemingly watching them. The group chuckled as it turned its head this way and that and almost upside down.

"I don't know if we are that interesting or if he sees his own reflection and thinks it's another seagull," remarked Marge.

Rita, meanwhile, took out her camera and successfully captured the silly antics of the bird. "They do grow them big out here, don't they?" stated Rita. "In Minnesota, our seagulls are half that size."

Claude explained that the gulls in Minnesota are actually lake gulls but these were real seagulls. Bigger body of water thus bigger birds."

"Oh, I see," said Rita.

Marge wasn't sure he was correct, but her friend seemed to believe whatever this gentleman told her. Once again, it reminded her how naïve and gullible Rita was.

As the sun slowly set, the lamps around the pier of the restaurant lit up and created a soft glow. The hostess came by and started the stout candle under the glass cover in the center of their table. The flame illuminating their faces and reflecting in the window changed the atmosphere to one of coziness and a bit of romance. This suited Rita and Claude just fine, but Marge was now a little uncomfortable. She did not want to appear ungrateful for the fabulous meal but also not wanting this "date" to become anything more. She suggested that it would be good to head back and check in with Marvel and Kitty.

*****

Just as the movie was rolling the credits and playing the final music, they could hear their friends returning from their evening out. There was a knock at the door and then the other pair peeked in.

"Are you two still awake?"

In they came with wide smiles. Rita sat on the bed alongside Kitty. Marge pulled up the desk chair.

"Well," Marvel inquired, "did you have a nice time?"

"The food was phenomenal," stated Marge.

"We had a gorgeous view of the bay and saw a breathtaking sunset," Rita added.

"You girls should see the size of Seattle's seagulls. They are huge! We had one right outside our window where we were sitting. It appeared almost as large as an eagle!"

"Rita, you are exaggerating a little," corrected Marge.

"How was the company besides the birds?" Kitty said, deadpan.

"We had a very entertaining time. Thank you, Rita, for including me."

After recapping their evenings, Marvel politely shooed them out of her room so she could get ready for bed. Her foot was throbbing so she was getting a little cranky.

The others said good night and shut her door behind them. It was relatively early and they weren't tired enough to go to bed so they strolled down to the common area on the hotel lobby. There they found a foursome playing bridge and two others with a checkers game on the table. Seeing an open table, they grabbed a deck of cards and sat. As they were getting situated, another woman approached their table.

"Hello, my name is Maryann. Would you mind if I joined you? My husband is watching some sports game, and I don't know the difference between a football and a baseball."

"Yes! Please sit down." Kitty motioned to an empty chair.

"Perfect! Now we have four. That opens up more options of games to play," Marge said happily.

"Do you girls play five hundred?" asked Maryann.

"I'm still learning," shared Rita, "but I'm willing to play if you ladies don't mind playing with a rookie."

So it was decided that Maryann would be Rita's partner. She assured her that she was hard to beat and would teach her some finer points of the game.

Kitty looked over at her partner and exclaimed, "I believe we've just been thrown a challenge. A little wager, my friends?"

Maryann's eyes sparkled as she responded, "Oh yes, indeed. Count me in!"

Into the late evening, they played. They were having so much fun getting to know Maryann. She and her husband Frank were married quite young, had two children, and divorced while the children were in early grade school. Yet fifteen years later, they remarried after having spent time together chaperoning their son's prom! Now here they were, twenty years later, still happily married. Realizing they were the last bunch in the common room, they glanced at their watches and were surprised at the late hour. They played their last hand and added up the score. Maryann and Rita (with her beginner's luck) won. Saying good-night, they made their way back to their rooms.

*****

The LWC gathered the next morning in the common dining area. Marvel shuffled to join them, her foot able to fit in her sneaker but the purple and blue still visible above the shoestrings. Still, she was walking, and that made her happy. The friends, enjoying some delicious Seattle coffee and some apple Danish, filled Marvel in on their card game.

Just as they mentioned their new friend, Maryann and her husband approached them. She introduced them all to Frank. He was a ruggedly good-looking man who appeared, by his tanned complexion and heavily lined face, to have lived a great deal of this life enjoying the outdoors. Like his wife, he was friendly and had an easygoing manner. Maryann turned to Marvel and commented that she had heard about her tangle with the garment cart and hoped her foot was doing better today. Marvel, not one to wallow in her discomfort, lifted her foot up to demonstrate how it still fit in her shoe. Although colorful, it was not about to keep her from enjoying Seattle.

Originally, the friends had thought if the weather was kind to them, they would go the hour drive to the Mount Rainier National Park for some nature sightseeing. However, considering Marvel's lameness, they decided to alter their plans. Frank mentioned to the ladies that the zoo had some unique animals and venues and they could always grab a wheelchair if Marvel's foot began to hurt or swell too much. Maryann and Frank were off to do some shopping and visit the underground city.

"Underground city? What on earth is that all about?" questioned Marvel.

Frank went on to explained to the LWC that in June 1889, a fire destroyed the city of Seattle. The original city had often flooded so the leaders decided to rebuild Seattle a story or two higher than the original street level. He continued in 1965. A local citizen realized there might be interest (and profit) in the subterranean ruins. He established Bill's Speidel's Underground Tour. Now tourists come to hear tall tales from Seattle's history as they tour the underground city. "Which is precisely what we are going to do today. We'll let you know it we find it worth the price of admission."

"Frank loves history and mystery," Maryann shared as she lay her hand on his arm and cocked her head toward him.

"Enjoy then. We'll want to hear all about it!"

The LWC decided to rent a vehicle for the rest of their stay. After breakfast, the girls climbed into their small SUV and headed to the zoo. By now, the sun was shining bright and wisps of clouds floated lazily in the sky. They drove down near the pier where they could see the many huge ships coming and going with their cargo. Kitty recalled the conversation they had with the gentlemen they met on that last evening on the train and the discussion of exporting.

Rita spoke up. "I don't know anything about importing and exporting, but my oranges come from Florida. Does that count?" They looked over at Rita and shook their heads.

"That's probably as much as any of us knows," replied Marvel.

As they approached the Woodland Park Zoo, they could hear some of the animals talking. They heard the seals barking, no doubt for fish treats. One of the lions or tigers seemed to be presenting his position about something, and they heard the loud screech of birds. The zoo's entrance was filled with pictures of the animals they would visit inside. It was a large zoo so they took a colorful map with a ledger to figure out where they were and where they wanted to go. Right inside the gates was a large gift store that had many different keepsakes. They went to the guest service desk where Kitty took the initiative to check on wheelchairs. Looking at Marvel's foot, she decided to rent a chair now and save on the injury. Marvel started to put up a fuss, but Kitty put on her stern teacher expression and pointed to the chair. Marvel complied.

The zoo housed a wide array of animals from all around the world, many not seen in other zoos in the country; which made this zoo a special attraction. Woodland Park Zoo was made up of large natural habitat exhibits for each of the different animal species. It was beautiful to see all the extraordinary plant life and made it a little easier to envision where the animals would be like living in the wild. Pushing Marvel in the wheelchair made it easier to get to places. Each of her friends took turns pushing her. Upon entering the zoo, they were surrounded by the grasslands of a rural East African village. Looking at their map, they saw that here they would see hippos, giraffes, monkeys, and large cats.

When they came to the ocelot's exhibit, they found an elegant small version of a clouded leopard. The predator had large eyes, taking up most of its triangular face, with a dark border around them. At the back of its black ears was large white spots, and the tail was long and narrow with black bands. The women could see why these gorgeous cats were kept as pets, at one time by the rich and famous. As they were watching the graceful cat, some grade school children approached the exhibit. One of the boys leaned over the barrier and caught the cat's eye. The boy ducked below the wall and then peaked over it again. Now the wild cat moved over for a better view. The boy did this peekaboo game several times. Now the ocelot sat up on its haunches, watching with great interest. The boy, realizing it now had become a game, jogged a little further down the wall and disappeared below it. Popping his head up, he was delighted that the cat followed him and was waiting. The interaction was adorable and playful as if the ocelot was just a large house cat. Marge snapped a couple of pictures of the lanky feline and the young boy playing.

The friends caught a trolley that carried the visitors throughout the zoo. They decided to ride it to the far side of the zoo and make their way back. When the trolley dropped them off, they found themselves in front of the northern trail. Here they would see animal residents of the Alaskan tundra. They recognized the elk immediately and the majestic wolves. They stopped to watch the mountain goat as none of them had ever seen these large cloven-hooved beasts before. They were amused as the babies would crawl on their mother's backs and stand as if on lookout while she laid in the sun. A couple of the babies jumped and ran as if playing tag, shaking their heads and kicking up their heels. On the other side of the trail was the land of Australasia, made up of species from Australia, New Zealand, and islands of the South Pacific.

"I've always wanted to see kangaroos!" Marge said with a broad smile.

"And I've always wondered about those funny birds. You know, the one in the song. What were they called? I forgot," said Rita.

"Oh, I know, kookaburra!" Marvel began to sing, "Kookaburra sits in the old gum tree, counting all the monkeys he can see."

Kitty joined in, "My students always loved to sing this song and make funny gestures as they sang."

With that, they ventured down the trail to get a glimpse of the pouched animals and variety of colorful birds. As the day waned into the late afternoon, the LWC decided they had seen and done all that they could take in for one day. They stopped in the gift shop and found little tokens to bring home to their grandchildren. Pleasantly, they said goodbye to the gate keepers and headed to their rental car. Driving was proving to be a bit of a rub between them as they had different ideas on who should drive. Because of Marvel's injured foot, it was obvious she wasn't going to drive them back to the hotel so she climbed into the back seat. Kitty refused to sit in the back regardless of who was driving. She claimed it made her feel ill. Secretly, the others wondered if it wasn't more about her feeling in charge and being able to direct when she wasn't driving but said nothing.

They were about to pull out the coin to flip and decide when Kitty said, "Marge, you drove out here. Why not let Rita drive us back?"

Just like that, it was settled, and Rita crawled behind the wheel. Rita pulled out of the parking lot as Kitty, reading the map, relayed where to turn. As they were busy discussing the many beautiful and somewhat strange animals they had seen, Rita found herself on an on ramp that lead to a four-lane highway. Kitty noticed first and raised her voice to Rita. "We are on the wrong road!"

Rita, flustered, replied, "I didn't mean to. I just followed the lane we were in and it turned out to be an on-ramp!"

"It's fine. We'll just get off at the next exit," Marge stated sensibly.

Unfortunately, they were now entering a road construction area. There were cones dividing the lanes with signs showing upcoming curves and bends. It was a confusing mess even if one was familiar with the area. Of course, they were not.

Rita was leaning forward and griping the steering wheel so tight that her knuckles were turning white, following through the cones that she thought were going where she wanted them to. A car went past them. Its driver was waving at them and seeming to be saying something. Rita waved back. Then another car was driving toward them, and they were pointing and waving. Rita waved again, saying, "These Seattle folks are quite friendly, aren't they?"

At this moment, Kitty turned and yelled at Rita, "You are in the wrong lane and going the wrong direction! The concrete barrier should be on our left side, not the right!"

As more cars approached and swerved around them Rita held up both her hands, replying to the other drivers, "I know! I know! So sorry! I'm sorry!"

In the back seat, Marvel and Marge grabbed the headrests in front of them, yelling to Rita about going this way or that to avoid the oncoming cars. Kitty kept yelling for Rita to keep her hands on the wheel. Regrettably, the way the construction site was set up, there was nowhere for them to pull over or turn around.

Coming slowly toward them now with his lights on was a police car. He was stopping the oncoming traffic. Another police car came up behind them. He motioned for the LWC car to stop. Rita stopped the car right in the middle of the road as she was instructed. A seasoned patrolman came to the window and bending down looked inside the car. All four ladies smiled sheepishly at him. It was all he could do to keep down a chuckle. Requesting Rita's driver's license, he decided to ask how they had come to be driving down the wrong way. They all began to speak at once so he held up his hand to quiet them and get them to respond one at a time. After listening to their opinions of what happened, he handed Rita back her license and told them that since no one was hurt, he would just let things be. He told them he would help them turn their car around and get back to the road they wanted to be on. Now they could hear the honking horns from the cars waiting to get through. With the policeman's assistance, they carefully got the car going the correct way and followed the black-and-white car back to where they needed to be. They all waved thank you and continued on their way. The women didn't say much to one another until they reached the correct highway back to the city.

Rita was the first to break the silence. "Kitty, you know that all happened because you weren't navigating like you were supposed to."

Kitty spat, "What? You've got to be joking! You weren't paying attention to where you were going."

Angrily, they both faced straight ahead. Marge and Marvel exchanged a concerned look, not knowing what to say.

Finally, Marvel said, "Girls, I think we are all a little tired. We are in a new city, trying to figure out streets and then to add construction. Well, I think we just chalk it up to another one of our adventures! Yes, I am certain that as we think about how that last scene played out, we'll laugh. I mean, really. Rita thought the other drivers were all being so friendly by waving at her."

Rita glanced in the rearview mirror and gave her backseat companions a slight smile.

18

The meeting aboard the train between Stan, Claude, and Gunnar had not been coincidental. The men knew one another through business dealings and had arranged to meet on the train prior to arriving in Seattle. That the other passengers joined them proved an even better cover. This afternoon, the three men met at a cigar bar to confer on their business transactions. Stan congratulated them on meeting the women and teased Claude about his romancing Rita. Claude took it good-naturedly and commented that life shouldn't be all business without pleasure. Gunnar agreed.

Claude and Gunnar began their lives as underprivileged, but their father had been a creative entrepreneur who eventually found financial triumph. He started numerous different companies over the years and led them all to success. The first major achievement had begun as he was searching for a solution to a leaky car motor issue. Since mechanics were so expensive, he decided to find a way to fix it himself. He ended up creating the gasket made from rubber, and the idea took off. Suddenly, he and his young family were no longer living in a cramped rental house but moved out to the countryside with several acres to call their own. After this invention's success, their father realized he not only had a knack for inventing, but also for running a business. He employed a hands-on approach to marketing, production, and sales. It wasn't long before he branched out and developed other gadgets until his company grew into a Fortune 500 business. Under their father's tutelage, the boys learned the art of being suave businessmen. They had done well and lived comfortably, but that hadn't been enough to satisfy the brothers.

Claude had been married once for only a brief time. He freely admitted that he had been caught unawares by the lovely co-ed who caused him to lose his focus in his senior year in college. They were married right after graduation and quickly had two children. Before he realized their bank accounts had taken a swift downward turn, she had left him and the children. She had been after his money all along. Suddenly a young single father, he vowed never to be taken advantage of in any way again. If anyone would be pulling a con, it would be him! Never willing to share this dark chapter of his love life with others, he would tell people he had been widowed at a young age. Gunnar married his childhood sweetheart. She had been a saint and quickly became a hands-on aunt to Claude's two small children. Although she and her husband tried to introduce Claude to wonderful women, he steadfastly refused to be interested. As long as he had a loving extended family and terrific nannies for his children, he was set to face life without a mate. So far, he had succeeded.

Oh, there had been countless women in and out of his life. Some of the women were very lovely, but to Claude, they were just filling a space in his life to fulfill a purpose for a time then he would quickly dismiss them when they began looking for a future with him. He thought about Rita. She was an unusual choice. She was cute, but not what one would call pretty. She was outgoing, talkative, and friendly. Her outlook on life was generally simple and optimistic. He smiled to himself as he recalled how she told him how she likes to keep up with clothing trends, not wanting to appear an "old woman," and secretly subscribed to magazines to remain current.

Mentally returning to his meeting, he listened as Stan laid forth his plan. It was to be completed by the end of their stay in Seattle. Each man knew his role and what was expected of him.

"Are we all on board?" asked Stan.

Claude answered with a big smile, "Sure thing. This one should be a breeze!"

*****

That evening, the brothers and Stan met Rita and Marvel at a nearby restaurant with a patio surrounded by lilacs and other flowering bushes that kept them somewhat secluded from the outside world. Kitty and Marge decided on a different venue.

Immediately, Gunnar noticed Marvel walking with a slight limp and inquired what happened as the ladies took their seats. Without further encouragement, Rita began the story of Marge's mishandling of the suitcase caddy and how it had run over Marvel's foot. The gentlemen tried to look concerned as they covered their mouth to hide the slight grins on their faces. Somehow they knew it had been a comedy of errors and were imagining the scene. Next, the ladies told them about their trip to the zoo, leaving out the confusion of trying to drive home. After sharing their visit to the zoo, the conversation turned more personal. Stan asked the women about their families and what they did before retirement.

Marvel happily chatted on about Al and their three children, two daughters, and one son. Two of her children, now with families of their own, lived away. Her oldest son and his family lived in the Chicago area. It was a day's drive away for her. It was hard for her as she wanted to be as involved in her grandson's life. Her youngest lived a little closer, about three hours away on an acreage where they had a menagerie of animals. The beautiful land and the responsibility of taking care of the animals kept her four grandchildren busy yet they still found time to participate in band, sports, and other extracurricular activities. Marvel shared how she loved to spend time at their place and stayed as active with the kids as her aging body would allow. She proudly added that she could still ride a horse. Her middle child lived in the same city as she did, which was a godsend. It allowed her to maintain her home and yard with the help of her daughter's family. Her two grandsons, now both in their teens, kept her yard mowed, raked, and shoveled when the snow fell. The eldest of the two made the varsity hockey team this year, she shared enthusiastically. All were happy and safe, which is what gave her the most joy.

Stan pressed a little about her husband Al, what had been his career, what sort of activities he enjoyed or they enjoy together. Since he seemed attentive, Marvel found herself telling them more about herself and Al. Al had been a businessman through and through. He had begun in sales and had worked hard, often traveling on business for up to two weeks at a time. Eventually, his dependability, determination, and relational skills with customers got him noticed by those in higher positions and was rewarded with a real office. No more sharing a room with several desks and one overworked secretary for them to rely on. Marvel's memory briefly took her back as she remembered that day with clarity. The pride was evident on her husband's face as she and the children met him that first week in his new office for lunch. She dressed them up in their Sunday's best for the visit. She knew her husband had been proud to show them off. The kids were all over his office. Her son was sitting in daddy's big desk chair, swinging back and forth with only the very tip of his toes touching the ground. She added that he faithfully worked for the same company for thirty-seven years. When his ideas began to be passed over for younger men and experiencing that disappointment several times, he decided to retire.

Gunnar commented, "I hope the company took good care of him and your family when he retired and his eventual passing."

Marvel nodded, saying that she had been blessed by the company's pension as well as her husband's smart investments. Gunnar and Stan inquired about the stocks they had invested in. Without thinking, Marvel rambled on answering their numerous questions. She said that they lost some of their savings due to the high cost of caring for Al, but they had made some educated decisions so she lived comfortably and well. The men all smiled with kindness. Stan reached over to lay his hand on hers and told her she was a lucky woman to have had such a wonderful husband. She felt herself start to get a little teary but chose to stay composed. It was nice to have the company of men again, ones who really seemed to care and listen. She felt an old nagging feeling surrounding her heart, the ever present loneliness for Al. The conversation stalled briefly but after a moment, Stan turned to Rita, asking her similar questions about her family and husband.

Rita told them how the gregarious Howard (or Howie) swept her off her feet when she was very young. She chose to be a homemaker while Howie went to work for the family business, which was auto mechanics. Her Howie was a genius when it came to fixing anything with a motor! They had two children, a son and a daughter. Both lived within an hour or less distance from her now. Her son was yet to be married but had a steady girlfriend that Rita really liked. She remained hopeful the two would tie the knot. Her daughter, before starting a family, had begun her career working in the very exciting life of politics. She married when she was in her thirties and now had two grade school children who were the light of Rita's life. Rita was a very present grandma as her daughter returned to work full time and needed the assistance.

Suddenly, Rita remembered Claude and hoped he wasn't put out about how she had gone on about her late husband. If it bothered him, he certainly didn't show it. In fact, he asked her more questions regarding things she and Howie had liked to do together. Once again, the men seemed sincere and happy to hear all about their lives. Cheerfully, yet a little shyly, Rita went on about learning to play golf so she could tag along when Howie played. She admitted she never was very good at the driving but had become a decent putter. Howie had seemed pleased with her dedication. Then she caught the men and Marvel completely off guard by revealing that she and Howie had been avid motorcycle riders and had developed a group of friends that they had often ridden with on day trips.

"We called ourselves the Hot Mamas and Papas"

Astonished, Marvel exclaimed, "What? How could I never have known that about you?"

Rita smiled demurely. Claude's jaw was still a jar. This woman was full of surprises. Again, Stan asked about any stocks she and Howie had or other investments. Rita admitted she didn't really understand much about any of that so the family lawyer oversaw that part of her financial records. She shared that Howie tried to explain it all to her and get her involved but her brain just didn't work like that. Eventually, he gave up trying to teach her but always made sure she knew who and where to go if she had questions.

Stan replied, "Well, ladies, one of the reasons I was asking is because that is somewhat of a hobby—or better yet, a side business of mine: financial planning, investing, and educating individuals regarding the market."

Rita commented, "I wouldn't even know where to begin to ask you questions!"

Reaching into his sport coat, he removed his wallet and then took out two business cards, handing one to each lady. "We can talk another time. I'll even go over your portfolios to see if you are making the wisest use of your investment money. No charge."

Glancing it over, they quietly thanked him and placed it in their purses.

A knowing look passed between the men, but Claude was sensing his heart wasn't in it this time.

19

After a couple of days staying in the hostel, the LWC were moving on to another location. Their bags were packed and loaded into their rental vehicle as they headed to the Roosevelt Hotel, an appealing older hotel that was in stark contrast to where they had just stayed in. They wanted to have a variety of experiences on their journey.

Since there was a several hours gap of time from when they had to check out, the LWC had decided to drive to nearby Green Lake, which was a popular place, especially on a nice sunny Seattle day. It was a good-sized lake that was surrounded by a paved path, grassy areas to lounge on, and a sandy beach. There were many people walking their dogs, rollerblading, biking, running, and many others sitting in the grass reading and enjoying the sunshine. The friends had planned a picnic and stopped by a grocery store that had a deli to buy the food and beverages. They found an empty picnic table under some trees with a clear view of the lake.

Marvel and Rita were unpacking the sacks as Marge and Kitty went to find the porta-potty. When the two returned, they found a lovely display of their food and places all set. As they sat down on the bench seats, they felt something soft under the table. Rita let out a surprised gasp when something wet touched her toes. Somehow without seeing her, a small dog had wandered over and was searching the ground for any crumbs. Apparently, she liked Rita's toes as she was licking them. Marvel reached down and picked up the pup. She had happy, large, dark eyes; ears that looked like they were supposed to stand up but the tips folded over, fur that was soft and silky, and a little tail that wagged wildly. She licked Marvel right on the tip of her nose.

A young woman approached them, apologizing for her dog. They learned the pup's name was Harlow, named after the famous Hollywood actress, Jane Harlow, the owner's grandma's favorite actress. Harlow's owner's name was Rhoda. She was lying down on her blanket studying and hadn't noticed her dog had gone out. Since the ladies had plenty of food, they asked Rhoda to join them for their picnic. She hesitated at first but upon the insistence of the women, she sat down with them. Harlow was especially happy to be joining the picnic. She lay under the picnic table politely, her tongue panting slightly and waiting for any accidental or purposeful crumbs sent her way. The lucky dog was surrounded by soft-hearted souls who just couldn't keep from losing tidbits of food to the grass below. Rhoda shared that she was in her second year in grad school at the University of Washington. She had done her undergrad schooling in Ohio and felt it was time to venture out. She had always heard about the Pacific Northwest and how beautiful it was but had never seen either mountains or the ocean. So here she was. Her lunch mates gave her nods of approval as she told them her story. With appetites sated, the ladies began to clean up their plates and pack away what food was left. Rhoda and Harlow said goodbye and headed back to study.

Looking at her watch, Marge told them they still had time to fill before they could check in to their hotel. It was such a lovely day that they decided to go for a drive and take a broader look around the city and surrounding area. Kitty took the wheel and Marge was designated as the navigator. They had been wise choosing a vehicle to rent. They needed space for their luggage, something easy enough to get in and out of but not too low or too high. The car had all sorts of new *thingamajiggers*, as Kitty called them. Most of them, the ladies were uncertain as to how to use. The gentleman who rented them the car had given them a brief lesson on all the extra bells and whistles, but they were a little worried to push too many buttons. They weren't even willing to try the GPS. Marge had her map of the Seattle area out and was guiding Kitty back toward a main road. As they wound their way through neighborhoods, they saw small yards and so many of the houses built on hills. Many of the houses had flowering trees and bushes. Most of the side streets had roundabouts, which could sometimes prove confusing if you weren't sure where you were going. The backseat drivers were sharing their advice as they went that Kitty glanced often in the rearview mirror to give them her a "would you just be quiet" look. But it was to no avail as they were sure they were helping. Just before Kitty was about to pull the car over to give them a piece of her mind, they reached highway 5. She blew out a long aggravated sigh. Maybe the four had been together too long and needed a break. She'd have to think about this for a while.

Now on the freeway, they wondered where to go next. On the map, Marge saw the Washington Park Arboretum not far from where they were. She suggested it to her companions and all were elated with the idea. With Marge's navigation and a little help from road signs, they found their destination without any incident. Within the arboretum were separate parks from different geological areas, and the Japanese Garden was a premier attraction. The parks were divided mostly by plant species. There was the Woodland Garden that was made up of various types of trees from the dogwood to the Japanese maple and numerous trees located there had eye-catching foliage any season of the year. One garden they were excited to stroll through was the Pacific Connection Garden. This garden was cleverly made up of tree and plant species native to the five continents bordering the Pacific Ocean. It would be a small taste of what one would find in Cascadia (a term they learned was for the region near the Cascade Mountains), Australia, China, Chile, and New Zealand. The arboretum was large. With Marvel's injured foot, they decided to visit the Pacific Connection Garden first then just take in what they could. Each country had its own area within the twelve acres of this garden. They slowly made their way through the various parts where they saw many displays of color.

By the time they had walked through this portion, Marvel indicated that it was time for her to sit a spell. Not wanting to hold her friends back from seeing more of the gardens, she insisted they go on without her. She would be happy taking in the beautiful scenery around her and watching the people go by. Marge and Rita really wanted to see the Japanese Garden. Kitty felt she wanted to do some strolling and observing on her own. So the friends split up, setting a time to return to Marvel. As they made their way into the Japanese Garden, Marge and Rita were captivated with the beauty surrounding them. Even though it was still spring, the garden seemed to have been painted colorfully by an artist. There were blooming trees throughout the paths, flowers making their presence visible, and even the animals added shades of color. There were sunbathing turtles up on some rocks; ducks swimming in the ponds; and, of course, the orange, black, and white of the Koi fish, which reminded them of large goldfish. They watched as some children were leaning over some rocks and feeding the large bright fish. The fish would come right up to the surface and take the food from the children's hands. The children then would giggle out loud.

Kitty had chosen to walk toward the waterfront trail. Looking up the trees overhead, she saw some blue flowers that wafted a lovely scent. She read the sign nearby and learned that these were Chinese empress trees. Closing her eyes, she took in the fragrance and the gentle breeze blowing through the leaves. Taking out her phone, she backed up a little to get a better picture of the stunning scene. Moving down the trail, Kitty thought of Harley. She didn't allow herself to think about him much. They had had a good run together. He had told her toward the end of his clear memory. She wasn't one given to great sentimentality, being Norwegian, she guessed. She had remained strong throughout the curveball that life had thrown her husband. She was, however, fiercely protective of those she loved and had remained steadfast with Harley until the Lord called him home. She had been an ever vigilant caretaker of her man. She thought about how he would have liked this place. He had always had a great admiration for God's creation and had so enjoyed working in their yard and anything where he could be outdoors. She thought about the trees he had planted each day one of their three children were born. She smiled to herself, noting that for all her lack of sentiment, her husband had more than made up for it. She used to tease him that he was one of the children himself. He had such a hard time saying no to his kids, she had to be the disciplinarian. Often he would advocate on their behalf when they showed good behavior while under punishment. As if she thought being grounded from television for a week or missing a weekend of being with friends was so harsh. His eyes would get so big and pleading, and he'd give her his special little smile when he was negotiating for any of the kids. These were some of the things she missed about him, which began when he started slipping into the black hole of Alzheimer's disease.

Kitty was a wise woman who faced life head on. She never once thought of blaming God for what happened to Harley but she was mad at the disease itself. She had come to terms with it all and her friends had been a great source of help. Shaking her head, she thought about the Last Wives' Club. They would never had met if they hadn't all shared the difficult journey they did with their husbands. That certainly was a blessing that was a surprise. Now she thought they might be the closest friends she has had in a very long time.

You here with me, Harley honey? I feel like you are. I miss you holding my hand and swinging it back and forth with gusto. I miss you looking into my eyes and telling me that I don't always need to be so strong, that you had my back at all times. I miss you singing to me as you walked up the sidewalk at night after work. Darn it, Harley James! Why did you have to go and leave me? Sniffling a little, she opened her fanny pack and pulled out a tissue. *Okay, I'm through now. The children and I are good. Our grandson Jason reminds me so much of you, sometimes it hurts a bit to look at his handsome little face. Harley, thank you. You didn't leave me alone. You made sure others would have my back, and let me tell you, it takes all three of those women to do your job! To the moon, my love.* As she proceeded down the path, she caught a glimpse of bright yellow flitting among some branches. Looking up, she spied a goldfinch with his perfect little black beret on the top of his head. He seemed to be watching her. She smiled and kept walking.

They all met back where they left Marvel. There she was sitting on the bench and talking very intently to a chipmunk she was feeding. The little creature would cautiously reach out to her fingers holding a piece of fruit. Then it would hold it between its paws, chewing as quickly as possible to fit it all into its cheeks. Marvel had her camera and captured the moment on film. She was having a ball. Her friends all stood watching her for a moment then Kitty cleared her throat. The chipmunk darted around to get a better look at them but then looked back at Marvel, curious if there were any more treats. As the friends approached, it scampered off.

Sitting down next to Marvel, the friends rested a brief spell, looking at some of the cute photos Marvel had taken of her friend. Feeling ready to head to the hotel, they all made a final pit stop at the restroom located at the entrance and then piled in the car. Marge decided she would like to drive this time and said she knew how to get back to the hotel. As they drove along, they filled Marvel in on all they had seen. Kitty took out her phone and found the pictures of the lovely blue flowered tree and passed it around.

20

The hotel was just as they had hoped it would be. It had the allure of yesteryear with modern amenities. Since the hotel dated back to 1930, the lobby had an elegant, old-fashioned feel, and the rooms were not opulent but tidy and comfortable. The hotel sat in the heart of downtown Seattle, which made it convenient to walk to many locations. There were large department stores within blocks of the hotel, restaurants, a theater, and many shops providing local favor.

The women chose to share rooms so Kitty and Marvel headed to their room to unpack, as did Marge and Rita. Kitty preferred to be closest to the door so she plunked her things down on the first bed. This suited Marvel just fine as she then was closest to the bathroom. Immediately, she found her travel night-light and plugged it into the outlet next to the sink. Kitty picked up the remote and turned on the TV. The local news was on so they let it play as background noise as they hung up clothes and set their toiletries out. When the weather came on, Marvel sat on the end of her bed to pay attention. Good news, according to the weatherman, they were in for a couple of partly sunny days in the comfortable high sixties to low seventies. It would be the perfect weather for sightseeing and being outdoors. Mentioning this to Kitty, she asked what sort of things Kitty wanted to do over the next couple of days. Kitty didn't answer right away. Marvel prattled on about how she really didn't understand why so many of their friends flee to Southern states to live in their retirement. Minnesota was so beautiful with its four seasons and lakes. Sure, there were those unusual winters where they received a foot of snow at one time but it was mostly manageable, and she thought the amount of days below zero were highly exaggerated. She liked the winter months when things were so quiet when you walked outdoors in the parks or woods. What she didn't like would be the above ninety days with the claustrophobic humidity and the summer bugs.

Marvel stopped realizing she was the one doing all the talking. She turned to Kitty and said, "Kitty?"

"Oh, I'm listening, Marv. Just doing some thinking too."

"What about?"

"Us. Our trip."

"Why?"

"Let's wait until we are all together this evening or sometime soon."

"Okay, I guess."

There was a knock on the door. When Kitty opened the door, in came Marge and Rita. Marge sat on the closest bed and Rita sat down in the armchair. Kitty had finished unpacking and sat down next Marge. Marvel, still putting some clothes away in the drawers, asked what everyone wanted to do that evening.

Rita piped up first. "Since it is such a lovely night, why not go for a walk and just find a diner or something simple or get supper from a vendor?"

With their walking shoes on and jackets in hand, the LWC ventured out, mindful to check the street corner their hotel was on. As they began walking, they noticed several musicians putting on a show on the sidewalk. As they got closer, they realized the musicians were older men playing homemade instruments. One was playing a xylophone out of different size jars filled with different amounts of water, another was playing a drum seemingly made up of a pot with something stretched tightly across the top, and another played a flutelike instrument made from an old wine bottle! Amazingly, the music was good! People stopped to watch and listen, many of them clapping their hands to the music. Rita pulled out her camera and took several shots. Then continuing on their way, they spied a little diner so went in to grab a bite.

After ordering, Kitty spoke up. "Girls, I'm feeling somewhat *smothered*, for lack of a better word. For the past week or so, we have been mostly together, all four of us, and did everything together. I feel like I need a break or we need to do something different." The other three women didn't say anything at first but just kept looking at Kitty. She continued, "Even when I was married and had children at home, I would find I needed some alone time to recharge. That's it! I don't feel like I have an opportunity to recharge. I am not sure what the answer is but I needed to let you know how I am feeling before I blow up at one or all of you."

Now Marvel found her tongue. "I certainly understand, Kitty. I guess maybe that's what I'm feeling too. I need my alone time to 'recharge' as you put it. I feel like I'm running on energy fumes."

Feeling uneasy about this conversation, Rita wanted to know what they should do. She was one who loved being busy and being around others. She felt reenergized on this trip having constant companions, including Claude. She wasn't sure why but this revelation of Kitty's was hurtful. She chided herself silently. After all, Kitty was just being honest about her needs, but Rita couldn't help but wonder if much of this was directed at her. Was she jealous of Claude's attentions to her even though she told Rita to be careful? Was that just to cover her own feelings? Maybe she was just reading too much into what Kitty was saying. She just didn't know or understand.

Marge, being a longtime friend of Marvel's, wasn't surprised by what she had said. She was a bit amazed that Marvel lasted this long with constant companions. Over the years, she had known Marvel to retreat into her own cocoon from time to time, emerging days later refreshed and ready to partake in social activities again. She learned early on in their friendship not to take these stages personally. She guessed that Kitty was much the same way.

Before Marge was able to put in her two cents, Rita looked over at Kitty and blurted out, "Are you mad at me? Are you jealous that Claude is interested in me? Don't you like me, Kitty?" Dumbfounded, the three women looked at Rita with mouths wide open.

"What on earth!" declared Marvel. "Where did all that come from?"

Kitty looked crossly over at Rita. "Really, Rita? That's what you took away from my comments? You are unreal!" With that, Kitty got up from the table, set down a twenty-dollar bill to cover her uneaten meal, and walked out.

Rita's eyes filled with tears. She hated confrontation and couldn't stand when someone was mad at her.

Marge finally spoke up. "Rita, you are taking all this too much to heart. Kitty was just sharing what she needs right now. Not everyone is like you. In fact, Marvel is much the same way. Over the years, I have come to understand her need for solitude from time to time."

"I was going to suggest since you and I are already sharing a room, we continue to do so and that maybe for a few days, Kitty and Marvel each get a room of their own and do their own things."

Marvel leaned across the table and placed her hand on Rita's hand. "I think Kitty and I were able to stay together with you and Marge because you two have made things fun and we enjoy you. But having said that, sometimes being around people—anyone—with no break wears folks like Kitty and I down. We are just cut from a different fabric. It doesn't mean we are mad at you or don't like you. It just means our people gauge is running on empty, and the only way it gets filled back up is for us to 'check out of life' for a while. Rita, this even happened when we were raising our families. This is something we had to learn to work through in our marriages too. It is nothing personal about any of us."

Sniffling, Rita just responded with "Okay." Right then, their meals arrived. "So what do I do now that I spouted off?"

"Well, since I've known Kitty, you need to just give her some space for a bit. Then when the time is right, you can apologize, and I guarantee you two will be just fine."

"Rita, why would you ask Kitty if she was jealous of you and Claude?"

"Oh, I was just trying to think of anything I did wrong. I hate it when people are mad at me. Howie used to get all ruffled because I would apologize for some things that weren't my fault, but I just like everyone to be happy!"

"You do realize that isn't possible all the time, right?"

"I wish it were."

Marvel decided a topic change was appropriate and steered the conversation away from touchy subjects for the remainder of the meal.

21

Kitty found herself walking in a nearby park. In the center of the park was a round fountain. The water sprung up high before falling back into the pond below, making splashing noises and creating bubbles all around. She watched the water dance for several minutes, allowing no thoughts to enter her head. She needed to just be emotionless for now.

As she sat on a bench near the fountain, she began to look around the park. Just to her right was a piece of art that she now realized was a jungle gym. Next to it was what she thought was a large old tree with a thick trunk where children could climb. Its long, flowing branches had been trimmed over the playground. As she observed more closely, one of the tree's wide branches hung over some sand and saw that there were swings attached to it. She walked over to sit on one of the swings, slowly rocking back and forth while she took in the young children climbing and playing in the artfully made playground. A small smile formed at the corners of her mouth as she just allowed herself to be still.

*****

Once back at the hotel, Marvel did what Marge suggested and inquired about another room for a day or two. Fortunately, it not being actual tourist season yet, there was a room available. She quickly went up to the room she was to share with Kitty and left her a note. Then she repacked her things, placed them on the baggage cart, and went in search of her new abode. In her own room, Marvel unpacked again. This room had a king-size bed, a desk, and an armchair. In an armoire facing the bed was a television on a swivel, allowing it to be turned toward the chair or the bed. She was pleased to see that this bathroom had a bathtub so she set about preparing a bath to unwind.

Before undressing, she called room service and ordered a glass of wine and asked if they had any candles that she could use. Within ten minutes, there was a knock at the door. The server had a nice cold glass of Chardonnay and a couple of candles in holders for her. They even brought her a book of matches. With the tub filled to her liking, she placed the two candles in the bathroom, one on the counter and the other on the edge of the tub. She carefully lit them, placed her glass of wine on the counter, and undressed. Before slipping into the relaxing warmth, she made sure there was a towel nearby to dry her hands, her book, and the glass moved within easy reach from the bathtub. She dimmed the lights and stepped into the water. Laying her head back, she allowed the soothing warm water to settle over her. She closed her eyes and thought about the earlier conversation at the diner.

She herself was surprised that this minor blowup didn't happen sooner on their trip. Perhaps, she thought, it had to do with so many new things they were experiencing that kept her and Kitty going. Marvel shook her head absentmindedly, opened her eyes, and reached for her wine. The room had a soft glow, and the flame of the candle on the bathtub edge flickered with her movement. As she laid back again with her wine, she knew it was time for her to do a little soul-searching about her life and what might lie ahead. She had been avoiding it since losing Al. She had been content to live day to day, going through the motions since his death. She thought she had been dealing with it all well by immersing herself into her grandchildren's lives, but it dawned on her now that she had been merely running away from the hard reality. Present, but not really living.

She smirked at herself, knowing all too well that running away was her *modus operandi*. Al had known it too and would gently call her on it if he saw things becoming dismantled in her life. She recalled one time when she was working in an office after college and had somehow gotten into the middle of a tumultuous relationship between two friends. After several weeks of lies and backstabbing comments, she was finished. She called Al and told him she was quitting her job. Somehow he managed to talk her into staying until the end of the day without quitting and waiting until they could talk things over. She remembered their talk so clearly. The phrase that always stuck with her and kept her in check often was when Al told her that she was a teapot and continued to put up with negative things over and over until she finally had it and blew up in steam! How true his statement had been, and he was the only one who could have said that to her.

So, Al, sweetheart, we never talked about what I was to do when you left me. Oh, how I wish I had your structured thinking to bounce thoughts off of now. What would you have done had it been the other way around? I know you. You'd have missed me, but you would have bought a cabin somewhere and spent your time there as much as possible, fishing and hunting with your grandchildren. You would have had a plan. That never crossed my mind to think about. As long as I had you here on earth, things just seemed they would be taken care of. I had a purpose—that was you. I guess it never occurred to me that I would need a new purpose someday. She mused over these thoughts until the water had cooled significantly, never having opened her book. She got out to dry off.

When Kitty returned to her room, she noticed Marvel's note explaining that they were going to have separate rooms for a couple of days. She had a moment of regret concerning their earlier conversation but had to admit she was relieved. Contentedly, she picked up her knitting and propped herself up with pillows on her bed. Grabbing the remote, she said out loud, "Let's see if I can find a good movie."

Across the hall, Rita and Marge decided to get comfortable and changed into their robes and slippers. Pulling out a deck of cards from her bag, Rita sat at the table that sat near the window. As she shuffled the cards, she turned to Marge. "Marge, would you like to play some cards?"

Marge had already gone into the bathroom to start a bath. "Not right now. I'm going to take a bath and wind down a bit. That okay with you?"

"Of course! I'll just play some solitaire. Enjoy your bath."

Grabbing her book, Marge slid into the bathroom and shut the door.

Rita heard the running water as she laid out her cards to play alone. She tried to quiet her mind as she focused on the game, looking for potential moves. She was still upset about the dinner conversation, and she knew she could think herself into insanity if she didn't make herself stop. It crossed her mind that this trip might have been a mistake. "Oh, for goodness' sake, Rita Jane, stop being such a worrywart!" she scolded herself. "All will work out in the end. I must get over being so insecure. Howie would be giving me that look of his right about now."

22

Though it was true that Stan was in the import-export business, what he collected wasn't something that would be showing up on any invoices. Many years ago, he had legitimately been in a position where he traveled the world. During those business trips, he saw to creating his own business on the side, which eventually became profitable enough to go out on his own.

It was on a trip to Africa where he met the Pierson brothers. Through various business dealings, the men became friends and eventually joined Stan in his endeavors. The men thrived on the thrill of a job with high risks. They were masters of deception and convincing. They had imported many fine pieces of art, historical artifacts, and jewelry, though customs would never know it. Often prior to a delivery, they would keep themselves amused and make money by other means of deception. This was their plan this time.

The scam was well into operation. Claude, Gunnar, and Stan were sequestered in Stan's room, complete with computers and new disposable cell phones. This was one scheme that they could perform from anywhere and everywhere. Stan announced that the website was ready. The men gathered around the screen to see Stan's handiwork. They were looking at a darling puppy that the site claimed was in need of a new home because the owner had become critically ill and couldn't care for it. It stated that interested parties could either click on the e-mail link or call the phone number provided. Slapping Stan on the back with approval, Claude and Gunnar told him to send it out. With a click of a button, their newest ploy for people's money was in play. Within minutes, they received their first call inquiring about the puppy.

Claude would handle the pet calls as he had charm and his voice dripped with sincerity. He skillfully read the script, describing the puppy and situation and assured the caller that it was a good thing she called because the puppy's future welfare was unknown as it would be such a shame to have to surrender her to a pound. He explained that the pup had all its shots was good with children and other pets. The family didn't want any money for the dog, just that the new owner pays for shipping it to them. Claude expertly avoided questions of the dog's location. Through friendly conversation, Claude acquired all the information he needed on the caller to provide the answers that would draw the target in. Before disconnecting, he knew the woman's name, address, and credit card information. She was going to talk with her mother who she thought needed a furry companion. They agreed she would call back the next day, if not before, to confirm whether or not to ship the puppy. Of course, Claude would recommend a shipper who would require a certain pet container for the trip as well as whatever other equipment he could convince the woman to buy. But the truth was, the money would be sent and the buyer would wait and wait for a pup that would never arrive.

Hanging up the receiver, Claude smiled broadly and said, "Men, this is going to be as easy as taking candy from a baby. We should have used this gimmick years ago!"

Gunnar readily agreed as their website already had numerous hits and shares. Who can turn away from a darling puppy in need?

*****

The LWC all met for the Continental breakfast the hotel provided. Kitty was quietly drinking her coffee while the others chatted about the day ahead.

"What shall we do?" asked Rita.

The women all looked at their friend and smiled. Marvel answered first, "I think we should all do our own thing today, at least part of the day."

Marge and Kitty nodded their agreement. Rita looked from one face to another, trying to determine if this was just decided or not.

"Rita, if you don't want to do something alone, contact Claude."

With that, the three women stood up and cleared their dishes. Rita remained in her chair, mouth slightly open in surprise. "So what's a girl to do?" ruminated Rita as she slowly dialed Claude's number.

Claude didn't answer right away. Just when she was going to hang up, she heard his baritone voice. "Why, hello, Rita! How wonderful of you to call."

Rita felt herself blush as she explained she was on her own today and was hoping he was free. Disappointedly, Claude informed her that he was busy but thought he could get away sometime midafternoon. She wondered what he was busy with but felt she shouldn't ask. They decided to meet at the Space Needle later that day. With a happy sigh, Rita hung up. Some time alone might just be uplifting. Hoisting her purse strap over her shoulder, she cleared her dishes and headed out to do some shopping.

It was overcast but the sun kept peeking out from amongst the clouds. Marge decided to take a ferry ride to a nearby island. As she walked past the parked cars already on the ferry, she noticed that some of their passengers were still sitting inside. She spied a man taking a snooze and still others on the phone. She walked through the cabin and found the staircase that led up to the second deck. It was too nice a day to remain inside. Putting on her sunglasses, she bounded the stairs. Once topside, she leaned on the railing and looked out over Puget Sound, watching some large ships coming into port as well as small recreational boats zipping back and forth. Overhead was the constant chatter of seagulls as they flew near, looking for any goodies they could snag. She found a seat near the railing and sat down. She intended to read, but more and more people were filling up the ferry and she found herself content to people watch. Some wore business attire, and she wondered if they were going out to the island to do business or returning to the island after having concluded business in the big city. She knew that there was a decent-size population of people who lived on the island and had heard its small town had plenty to see. She was looking forward to the views from the ferry as they crossed the Sound and investigating the island.

Kitty was somewhat of a history buff so decided to take the underground city tour Maryann and Frank had told them about. Hopping on a bus near their hotel, she found a seat and read the brochure. She double-checked that her camera was loaded and that she had an extra film if she needed it. Pleased with herself that she remembered the film, she watched the buildings and people go by as they headed to her destination. She was grateful to have a day all to herself to do whatever she felt like. Although most of the time the ladies decided together where to go and what to do, it also became tedious to check in with them for all the decisions. Today was just what she needed. As she got off the bus, she thought she would go on the tour, find a cozy café for lunch, and then decide what to do next.

Marvel had taken the rental car so she could drive to some of the villages that surrounded Seattle. She found it so interesting that Seattle really didn't have suburbs *per se* as was the case back in the Twin Cities. Here, there were smaller communities that had their own downtown shops, restaurants, movie theaters, etc. *What a lovely idea*, she thought. Sometimes she felt her hometown was just too sprawling. One couldn't tell when one was in a suburb or another as they just blended together. As she drove around, she realized there were bikers everywhere. She had seen many individual riders and often groups moving together like a flock of sheep. She couldn't imagine biking in these parts since there were so many steep hills, but these folks didn't seem to mind. She admired their courage and fortitude but she was secretly very happy driving a car. Signaling her turn, she crossed the drawbridge to enter an a little community that her grandchildren would refer to as artsy. First, she drove around the couple of blocks that made up the hub to get an idea where she would want to start. She was delighted to find that they were having a flea market today. She found a shady space on the street and parked. Strolling down the sidewalk, she found a store that she thought looked like fun. The bell jingled when she entered the door. The shop smelled of apple and cinnamon issuing from a teapot of flavored tea offered to visitors served with bite-size scones. Marvel graciously accepted both. This store seemed to have a little bit of everything! She decided to begin in the back of the store and work her way forward. On the wall were a wide assortment of T-shirts with funny or sarcastic phrases. As she read some of them, she couldn't help but laugh out loud. She could think of someone for many of them. It was one of those moments she wished she was rich and could just buy fun items like this for people she knew. Chuckling to herself, she continued to slowly wander through the aisles, looking over the countless array of books, gadgets, and gifts.

Window-shopping as she made her way around the heart of Seattle, Rita couldn't help but admire the expensive tailored outfits she saw. She decided at one such shop to go in and take a closer look. She was greeted by a middle-aged woman who was steam-pressing an outfit behind the counter. Rita assured her that she didn't need any assistance as she was merely looking around at all the lovely clothes. Smiling, the clerk returned to her steaming. Glancing at a wool suit's price tag, Rita thought, *Oh my goodness! It would take one entire social security check to buy something in here.* She didn't want to appear like she didn't belong in such a place so she casually looked at a couple of other outfits before making her escape.

Continuing down the sidewalk, she could smell coffee and realized there were two different coffee houses on this block alone. The aroma reminded her it was time for lunch. Turning the corner to the next street, she discovered a small café tucked between an art gallery and a bookstore. Entering the door, she noticed this was a popular eating establishment as most of the booths and tables were occupied. She found a table for two in the far back corner and sat down then she realized she needed to order at the counter. Placing her jacket over the chair, she walked up to the counter to look at the menu written on the blackboard that hung on the wall. She decided on a turkey sandwich with all the fixings on wheat toast and, of course, a cup of coffee.

As Rita sat at her table, waiting to be called to retrieve her lunch, she contentedly watched the other patrons from elderly folks to teenagers. She was imagining that this little place had probably been in existence for many years, making it a hot spot for the locals. Just then, she heard her name and went to get her sandwich and coffee. She took time eating her lunch and sipping her coffee. She looked at the clock on the wall. She still had an hour to fill before Claude thought he could meet up with her. Sighing, she took another bite of sandwich. To her delight, her phone rang shortly after she finished her last bite. Claude was done early and ready to meet her. He had somewhere special to take her.

*****

As the evening approached, the women began returning to the hotel. Kitty, feeling a bit more rejuvenated, thought she'd wait for the others in the lounge, reading a newspaper. Marge and Rita arrived minutes apart and sat down near Kitty. It wasn't much longer before Marvel sauntered in carrying some shopping bags. She approached them, all smiles and waving the bags.

"Girls, I found some of the cutest shops and a great flea market! I can take you if you want."

Marge looked at the grandfather clock that stood proudly against the wall. "How about we catch up over a bite to eat? I haven't eaten much since breakfast!"

They all agreed. The concierge told them of an Irish pub just down the street that had good food. So off they went. Sliding into the booth, they all began to tell their day at once. This made them laugh. One would have thought they were old friends who just happened to run into each other! Marge waved her hand in the air and pronounced that they should take turns *after* they ordered. As they ate, they shared about their day.

When it came around to Rita, she told them about her shopping and then meeting up with Claude. She explained that he had been busy earlier in the day and when she tried to ask him about it, she felt like he brushed her off. "What do you suppose that was about?" she inquired.

"Well, maybe he is trying to add some mystery," Marvel suggested.

"Maybe he's up to no good," Kitty quipped.

"Oh, Kitty! Don't be that way."

Kitty rolled her eyes and shrugged her shoulders. "We'll see," she mumbled.

"I'm sure you're wrong, Kitty. When Claude and I met up, he took me to this handsome place with an unbelievable view at the very top."

"Where was it?" inquired Marvel.

"It's called the Smith Tower. It was the very first skyscraper in Seattle built in the early 1900s. Here, I grabbed a brochure." Passing the brochure of information over to Marvel, she continued, "It's so amazing to see the old elevators, which still work, and take the tour of the legends of that place. The top floor has a bar and lounge with a—Oh, what did Claude call it? Doggone it! I can't remember the phrase."

"Says here it's designed after a speakeasy of yesteryear," read Marvel.

"Yes, that's what Claude said! I need to take you guys there. It is pretty neat and, as I mentioned, has a phenomenal view."

"I'm game!" offered Marvel.

"Me too," joined Marge.

They all looked expectantly at Kitty who was reading over the literature. "Yes, seems really interesting. Count me in too!"

"I have one question. I was too embarrassed to ask Claude, but what is a speakeasy?"

Kitty responded first. "The term *speakeasy* originally referred to the illicit bars during the Prohibition. It was illegal to sell and drink alcohol so people started serving alcohol behind closed doors in secret locations usually only known to a chosen few. There were no signs and had fake entrances that were decoys for the real entrance that you could only enter if invited and knew the password."

"Wow, Kitty! You know a lot of stuff!" remarked Rita.

"I love history, especially American history. While other girls were reading *Little Women_*and such, I was reading journals and books about our country's history."

23

As the LWC sipped their after-dinner coffee, Marvel glanced around the room and waved. The others looked to see who Marvel could possibly know here. Sitting in a booth along the back wall was Roxanne and her husband Terry who they had met on the train in their last evening.

Giving a wave back, Roxanne got up and approached the women's table. "Hello! Are you all having a good time? Isn't this a pleasurable city?" she asked.

"Oh my goodness, yes!" they answered.

"Terry and I have been busy taking in as many sites as possible before we head back to the East Coast."

"Where are you from? I don't think I ever asked," said Kitty.

"We are originally from Raleigh, North Carolina, but now we live and work in the DC area. We keep a place a few hours away in Virginia as well, our weekend getaway from the craziness of DC."

"Virginia is beautiful horse country, I hear," Marvel commented.

"There is an abundant number of lovely horse farms," Roxanne informed her.

Terry now joined the conversation as he stood near his wife's side. "Ladies, I trust all is well?" They all nodded.

"Funny we should run into you since this is not a small city!" Marge commented.

"Oh, I don't know about that. We are all probably running in the same circles doing tourist things," he replied. "Have you bumped into any of the others from the train?" They filled Terry and Roxanne in on seeing Claude, Gunnar, and even Stan.

Roxanne smiled knowingly. "I'm not surprised to hear that. One only had to see the way Claude looked at you, Rita."

Rita shyly looked down, not knowing how to respond. They invited their friends to join them, but looking at his watch, Terry said they needed to be going. Waving, they left the pub. Finishing up their coffee, the ladies paid their bill and started walking back to their hotel. It rained lightly during their meal so the sidewalks were wet and the air smelled fresh as they made their way. They decided it was too nice outside to close themselves up in their rooms so Kitty led them to the park she found the other day. Her friends were enchanted at the clever sculptures made into a playground. Marvel, walking to the swings, reached into her purse and pulled out a handkerchief. She wiped off the swing's seat and climbed on. She loved to swing. Marge quickly did the same with another swing. Soon the two were laughing as they swung themselves higher and higher.

"Girls, please, whatever you do, don't go and jump off seeing who goes further," pleaded Kitty as she pulled out her camera, "or we'd be calling the paramedics!"

Marvel and Marge seemed transported back to their school girl days. They had shared many a heartfelt conversation while swinging. Important decisions had been made on swings like these. What to wear to the dance? Which boy should to date? How were they going to get through that chemistry class? Those conversations had seemed like the most significant life decisions at the time. Had they only known it would be one of the simplest times in their lives? Maybe that was why playing on the swings brought them joy even now. It was a reminder of the life journey they traveled and the comfort of lifelong friendship. What was that Girl Scout song? "Make new friends but keep the old. One is silver and the other's gold." Such true words.

Hearing a squeal, they all looked at Rita. She had climbed up on the slide and was on her way down. "*Weeeee!* C'mon, you three, give it a try!"

Marvel and Marge started slowing down. Kitty moved closer to snap some photos. Soon they were all taking turns going down the slide.

Several children with their parents came to the park and watched these grandmas acting like little girls. It didn't take too long before the children ran over to join them. One mom turned to her husband and remarked, "I hope that's me at their age!"

24

Their ship had come in, literally. Stan and Claude were at the docks, waiting for their goods to be unloaded. Several large containers were lifted from the ship by massive cranes and placed in a fenced storage area. Gunnar had gone into the shipping office to sign the papers needed to retrieve their items. It wasn't long before he joined the others to walk over and inspect their containers. Passing through the security gate, they showed the guard their papers and he directed them to their boxes. A worker met them, opened the first one, and then climbed on a skid loader to unload the crates inside.

As they were unloaded, Stan took a crowbar to open each one. Lifting off the packaging, they found different pieces of very early twentieth century furniture. Each piece was carefully scrutinized and inspected for their craftsmanship. They smiled at one another with approval. Scattered between a few authentic pieces were masterful replicas. They would be hard to spot even by the experts. Looking over the packing slips, they checked off each piece as it was uncovered. On the slips were codes for each item. These codes meant nothing to anyone but the three men. It told them which pieces contained special compartments where additional merchandise was hidden. That merchandise would not be accounted for here in the semipublic location. They would wait until all was stored in their own warehouse. The furniture was exceptional, but what lay hidden inside was the real treasure.

Having accounted for each piece of furniture, it was then loaded on a waiting semitruck that would take it to the rented warehouse. Overseeing the loading, Stan barked orders at the delivery men, making sure none of the items were damaged in the transport. The three men followed the truck to the warehouse. The building wasn't huge but was large enough for the truck to pull inside. As the truck entered and parked, Gunnar pulled the large garage door shut. They didn't need curious eyes looking in as they unloaded. Piece by piece, their special cargo was loaded off the truck and placed carefully in the section of the warehouse that had been set aside. When the truck bed was empty, Claude handed the delivery men a check and opened the garage door for them to depart. He waved a thank you and closed the door after them. Finally, the three men could uncover their hidden treasure.

Stan walked over to the kitchen hutch that had been delivered and opened the side cabinet. Using his two thumbs, he pushed on the back corners of the lowest shelf. He felt a pop and stepped back to look. Under the shelf, a small compartment was revealed. He looked back at Claude and Gunnar who were peering over his shoulder. Reaching into the opening, he pulled out several large uncut diamonds. Handing one to each man, they held them up to the light. Big smiles broke out on their faces. These had been worth the wait and worth the risk they were taking. Checking the packing slip, they quickly went to the pieces with hidden compartments carrying their sparkling items. When they had retrieved all of them, they looked over their score. They not only had diamonds, but also sapphires, rubies, and emeralds. All the stones were uncut yet they still glistened brightly in the light. The men couldn't help running them through their fingers again and again.

*****

Meeting for breakfast and being fully aware they would soon be back on the train, the LWC deliberated what to do with the little time they had to spend in Seattle. The time apart had done Kitty a world of good, and her spirits seemed rekindled. Marvel too. Rita, still not comprehending fully what happened, accepted it as part of her friends' personalities and tried hard not to take it to heart. They decided to take their car, do some more sightseeing, and just let the day happen.

Marvel took the wheel as she had a few places in mind for them to see. Driving away from the center of the city, she took them to a nearby community she discovered. "Girls, I have a little surprise for you," she cooed. "I think this is the right street," she added.

They drove up the steep road. Ahead of them at the top of the hill was a bridge crossing the road. When they were almost at the top of the hill, Marvel found a parking spot, and they got out.

"What in heaven's name? What is that thing under the bridge?" exclaimed Kitty.

"It's a troll!" announced Marvel.

Under the bridge was a large, rough stone carving of a troll. It had a hand on the ground with its fingers raised slightly. Marvel, feeling playful, ran and squeezed between the fingers, pretending to be caught. Rita and Kitty snapped pictures as they laughed and took turns posing on the statue. Marge climbed up to its nose but stopped short of climbing on it. Coming back down, her foot slipped and she tumbled to the bottom. Rushing over, her friends helped her sit up.

"Are you okay? Are you hurt?"

"I think I'm okay. I hit my hip pretty hard. I'm sure it will be colorful later today." The friends helped her up and brushed her off. She winced in pain as rubbed her hip and slowly began walking toward the car.

"Well, I say we move on to something safer, like maybe some shopping," Kitty suggested.

Piling back into the car, they said goodbye to the troll and drove off. Marvel drove them to the village she saw yesterday. To all their delight, the flea market was still going. She pulled into a nearby parking lot just as a car was backing out and promptly occupied the empty space. It was one of those hazy days that, although overcast, one still needed their sunglasses. Rita, forgetting her sunglasses, quickly grabbed her floppy hat from the back seat and placed it strategically on her head to shade her eyes.

The LWC was thrilled to find vendors of all kinds at the market. There never seemed to be a shortage of local artists hawking their wares of jewelry, pottery, paintings, and more. The venue took up two streets. They were told that the flea market was closed every other weekend during the spring and fall months. This just happened to be the opening weekend. Although it was still too early in the season for much produce, there were tents that sold local honey, jams, and spices and a booth dedicated to different flavors of jerky. Here the friends discovered the yummy treat of salmon jerky. All of them bought enough to bring home and share. Wandering from merchant to merchant, they would stop to admire people's talent and their ingenuity. It seemed there were no limits to what could be used to make art, jewelry, and helpful household items.

"One thing I am not is," exclaimed Marge, "I am not very creative."

"Why, that isn't true!" Marvel quickly corrected. "You are extremely imaginative with your baking skills. You've come up with all sorts of goodies that never would have crossed my mind and some beautifully decorated cakes, I recall."

"Well, you know what I mean. I'm not very artsy, but I don't mind. I think it makes me have a deep appreciation for all the folks who make beautiful and interesting things. Like you two," she stated, pointing to Kitty and Rita.

Checking each booth up and down the street, they slowly made their way to where they started. Each had found additional items to purchase; most were gifts to bring home to their families.

"My daughters and daughter-in-law are really going to like the fun and unique jewelry pieces I got for them," Marge commented.

"I'm thrilled to have found those funny T-shirts for my son and grandson. Wait until they get them in the mail. They are either going to think I'm hilarious or that I've lost my mind!" Marvel laughed.

All in all, it had been a successful outing. Now it was time for a snack. They found a little hole-in-the-wall ice cream shop that suited them perfectly. Having ordered their creamy treats, they looked for a place to eat. They found a booth and sat down for a spell. With only a couple days left in Seattle, they decided to make a list of things they would like to make sure to experience. Kitty pulled out a notepad and pen from her shoulder bag. Marvel remembered she carried the picture map of the city and took that out, smoothing it flat on the table to see places to visit. They checked off Pike's Place, the zoo, the gardens, the Space Needle, and a few other attractions one or more of them had seen. There were a couple of places where they had not visited that others recommended to see, the Seattle Aquarium, the Great Wheel, several parks, and, of course, a Sounders soccer game.

"What is the Great Wheel?" asked Marvel.

"It's that tall Ferris wheel that goes out over the water. Remember, we saw it when we were in the taxi?" reminded Marge.

"Oh, yeah! That might be fun. I imagine the view is superior," Marvel said.

"Not on your life! You all be daredevils if you want, but I have no desire to be helplessly going around high above the water. Virtually a sitting duck. Count me out!" Kitty firmly stated.

Marge smiled and assured Kitty that was one experience they would not partake in, at least this time around.

"I've heard many positive things about the Aquarium. I would love to see the playful otters and learn more about the fish from around here," offered Rita.

"I agree," added Marvel. "I'm wondering what lies underneath those waters. Since I'm not willing to suddenly learn to scuba dive, this would at least be a peek of the world below."

All nodded in agreement and finished up their ice cream. As they took their waste to the trash can, Kitty couldn't help but wipe off the table with her napkin. Her friends smiled knowingly, a left-over trait from teaching young children.

Marvel still had possession of the car keys. As they approached their vehicle, she hit the button to unlock the doors and open the back gate. Feeling a resurgence of energy from their treats, they quickly placed their shopping bags in the back and slid into their respective seats. As they buckled up, Marvel handed the map to Kitty who was riding shotgun and then hit the button for the gate to close. "I gotta tell you, some of the *extras* that this car has are kind of handy! But I still don't understand some of the new cars that don't even have keys. You push a button to start them."

Rita exclaimed, "How in the world does it not make it easy to steal the cars?"

"They have 'fabs' keys," informed Marvel.

"Oh, for goodness' sake!" Kitty rolled her eyes. "The device is called a key *fob*, and you cannot start the car unless the device is right there. My son-in-law's new car has that."

"I don't think that would be a good thing for me," Rita exclaimed. "I'm always locking my keys in my car so anyone breaking in could drive off with it!"

"Rita! It would be the same if someone broke in with your keys still in the car. Oh, never mind!" Kitty quipped and turned to Marvel. "Well, let's get going."

Marvel thought that it was a good thing they would be returning home. Kitty's patience with Rita was thin at best.

25

Upon reaching the Aquarium, the task at hand was finding a parking spot. One of the predicaments that they had observed in driving a car was how small and narrow the parking ramps were as well as each individual space. This was the part that Marvel dreaded the most, especially in a rented car that by no means was economy size. The first parking spot they saw was right next to a large cement pillar, which they didn't even dare to try and squeeze into, let alone trying to get out of the car once they were parked. Driving on, they finally found one that Marvel felt somewhat confident she could pull straight into and get back out of when they were done. They held their breath to slide themselves out of the barely open doors so as not to dent the vehicles on either side of them, but they managed. The group sighed with relief as they straightened their clothing and headed to the entrance.

Marvel, herself a nature lover, had a granddaughter who was captivated by marine life. She smiled a little smile to herself as she recalled helping when Carrie had been home ill and couldn't get enough of the animated film, *Finding Nemo*. They had watched it so many times that Marvel could recite the movie practically word for word. Still, as the grandma, she had treasured those few days of snuggling under a soft blanket as they watched together. Carrie insisted the movie be paused if Marvel had to leave the room.

As they got up to the counter to purchase their tickets, Marge grabbed a couple of the colored picture maps. Unfolding it, she began to look over the exhibits and plan on how best to see everything. Rita, looking on, was pointing out the places she didn't want to miss for sure. "Okay, okay. We'll get to it all, Rita. I promise," Marge assured her friend.

They walked past the gift shop, deciding they would check it out after they had been through the Aquarium. Marvel ventured ahead and was looking through a thick glass. As her friends drew near, she heard Rita exclaim, "Oh dear! What an odd-looking animal!"

"It says it is a giant octopus. He is rather *interesting*' looking, isn't it?" Marvel agreed, fascinated.

Kitty began to read aloud the plaque next to the tank that explained about the creature they were watching. Rita had had enough of the odd animal and moved on. When she thought of marine animals, she only thought of things like seals, whales, and those entertaining otters. In her mind, that octopus looked like it belonged in a horror movie. When she came upon the coral reef exhibit, she was happy to see brightly colored corals and fish. Here she waited for the others to catch up. The ladies made their way through all the displays, spending much of their time watching the otters wrestle, swim, and groom each other. They learned that there were two types of otter, the sea otter and the river otter. Both types could be found in Washington. As had become the norm, Kitty read the descriptions and information aloud. The others didn't mind. After all, once a teacher always a teacher. More than once, she commented how much she wished there had been something like this to bring her students to learn about sea life. She shared how children learn and absorb so much more when they can see and touch things to help them make a connection to the lessons. Marvel smiled at Marge and Rita. Kitty, when speaking of her past students, showed a warmer side to her than they were accustomed to seeing.

Rita picked up on it and said wistfully to her friend, "Kitty, I so wish my children had a teacher like you. Don't get me wrong, they had some wonderful instructors, but I can tell you care about the whole person and a bigger picture for their lives than just the academics."

"Yes," Marge added, "your pupils were very lucky indeed!"

Kitty smiled with gratitude and whispered her thanks. Marvel sighed gratefully. Maybe they were finally figuring out the ebbs and flows of friendship.

As they finished seeing all the exhibits, they ventured back to the gift store. The friends went inside to look at the different items for sale. Marvel found a stuffed Nemo for her granddaughter and picked out some postcards.

"Oh, good idea, Marv. I should get some postcards too," Marge said as she began to look through the different pictures.

As they paid for their purchases, they discussed what to do next. Soon they decided it was time to head back to their hotel. They were relieved when they got to the parking lot that one of the cars next to them had left so only the driver and passenger behind her had to hold their breath as they slid into the vehicle. Carefully, Marvel slowly backed out, unsure she could get out of the spot with one move. As she inched her way, her ever alert copilots were watching and giving directions. Finally, they were able to creep out of the ramp. Emerging from the exit, they turned down to a side street and went up a steep hill. This was nerve-racking for Marvel, especially since halfway up the hill was an intersection and a traffic light.

"Oh, I hate driving and stopping on these hills. Thank heavens our car is an automatic. Can you imagine trying to negotiate these things on a manual?"

"I definitely cannot fathom these hills in ice and snow!" added Marge.

"Maybe that is why Seattle has such a great transportation system. People don't want to drive up and down the hills," remarked Rita.

"Good point, Rita," Kitty commented.

Marvel stole a sideways glance and hid her smile. As they neared the hotel, they couldn't see an open parking spot. "I'll drive around the block and ask for Al's *magic* for a spot to open up," Marvel said.

"What magic?" inquired Kitty.

"Whenever we needed to find a good parking spot, Al would tell the children that he was going to use his magic. I'm not kidding when I tell you, somehow there would be a spot close to the entrance of wherever we were headed." Circling the block and approaching the hotel once again, Kitty's mouth opened. Just pulling out in front of the building was a sedan. Marvel put on her blinker and winked at her companions. "Thanks, Al!" she mouthed as she parallel parked in the vacated space.

They piled into the elevator, needing to freshen up. Marvel was telling them about the Nemo toy she bought for her granddaughter then the conversation turned toward the trip home. They couldn't believe they had been gone for two weeks already. They were all feeling the tug to see their kids and grandkids. It was time.

Just then, Rita's phone chimed. Pulling it out of the side pocket of her purse, she saw a text from Claude. He wasn't sure what her plans were on returning but he and Gunnar would be heading back the next day and was hoping he could see her for dinner. She looked at her friends and asked what they thought. She didn't need much encouragement to take him up on his offer. She was about to text him back when the phone rang. It was Claude. He wasn't sure she would see his message so he thought he'd call. He was thrilled she would have dinner with him but he invited all of them. He, Gunnar, and Stan would like to take them to dinner to celebrate their successful business trip. It was decided that they would meet at a fancy supper club, which Claude insisted upon would be the men's treat.

If Rita was disappointed that it wasn't just her and Claude, she didn't show it. Besides, she had been conflicted on what to do since she wanted to see Claude but also not miss their last dinner in Seattle with her friends.

26

It was a scenic view from their table in the restaurant. The clouds had begun to break up, and the sun made an appearance in time to say good night. The orange, peach, and pink hues stretched out across the expanse of the water.

The men had ordered champagne to celebrate with the ladies that evening. Gunnar was in a rare gabby mood and shared with the ladies about the incredible furniture they imported and how exciting it was to open the containers to reveal the contents. He explained that some of the pieces had already been sold to individual collectors and the others would be sold at or to antique furniture venues. There was one piece though that had really caught his eye and was trying to convince Claude and Stan to allow him to keep. It reminded him of his wife's (God rest her soul) grandmother's hutch.

The champagne arrived with some grapes and an assortment of cheese and crackers. Rita jumped involuntarily when the waiter popped the cork. Claude reached over, laying his hand on hers as he looked into her eyes and smiled. "To Seattle and success, as well as sharing a delightful evening in the presence of stunning beauty. Oh, and that goes for the scenery as well," toasted Claude.

He is smooth, Kitty thought as she watched her friend bubbling with joy. She just wished her gut wasn't telling her that there was more to the story of Claude and Gunnar than they knew. Still, she clinked glasses and added a hearty "Hear, hear!"

The meal arrived in courses; five of them, to be exact. Marvel stated she would have to buy a new wardrobe for the trip home because none of her clothes were going to fit anymore.

"Speaking of the trip home," said Claude, "when are you gals heading back?"

"Tomorrow," they answered in unison.

"Oh, well, I guess it's a good thing we got together tonight then. Will you be returning on the train?"

"Yes, we decided to take it both directions. To ride it out and then fly home was just too expensive," replied Marge.

"Will you be stopping anywhere on the way back?" wondered Gunnar.

"Maybe, but doubtful. A day trip or something, but it's time to go back home," explained Marvel.

"I see," said Gunnar. "I sort of feel that way too, but then I remember I'll be returning to an empty house. Not sure I want to face that."

"It gets easier," Marge promised.

"Stan, what about you?" Kitty inquired. "Are you missing your family?"

"Sure. I travel so much for work that the days and weeks begin to blend. That's when I know I've been gone too long. I'll be heading home soon too."

The group told stories, laughed, and did a few turns on the dance floor before the evening wrapped up. As the ladies were walking out, Claude pulled Rita aside and asked if he could meet her for breakfast before they headed out. Since the train wasn't departing until 10:00 a.m., she agreed to meet him in the restaurant in her hotel lobby at 7:15 a.m. As she stepped away to join her friends in the taxi, he lifted her hand to his lips and gently kissed it. She looked back at him and winked before closing the taxi door. The ride back to the hotel was quiet with all of them feeling content and relaxed. Rita finally broke the silence, telling the others that she and Claude would be meeting for breakfast. They all nodded and smiled at her, wondering if this would be the last time she would see the gentleman she had become smitten with.

Back in their room as they prepared for bed, Marge asked Rita directly about her feelings for Claude. Rita couldn't seem to find adequate words. She stumbled about saying how much she enjoyed his company but felt unfaithful to Howie. Then when she would think or talk about Howie, she felt somehow unfaithful to Claude. Finally, she turned to Marge and blurted out, "I have no idea what I'm feeling or if I should be feeling anything! What should I do?"

Marge wrapped her friend up in a warm hug. "Rita, you don't have to have it all figured out right now. Claude is a handsome, charismatic, and interesting. You have every right to be drawn to him. And on top of everything else, he appears to have great taste in women. He has sought your company, after all!"

"I just don't know. I have only loved one man my whole life and gave him my whole heart so many years ago. Does that cancel out when he leaves you for heaven?"

"*Hmmm.* Well, I don't believe it *cancels* your love for Howie, but I do believe our hearts are made to expand with each new person we choose to love. Look at how our love for our children expanded. We don't love one more than the others. Love just grows somehow. I didn't know Howie before he came to the home, but from what you and your children have shared about him, I know he would want you to be happy, however that looks, in your life after him."

"This is all so confusing. Nothing like Claude has ever happened to me before. Don't get me wrong, Howie was wonderful and I am proud to have been his wife, but he certainly wasn't wealthy, worldly, or turned heads where ever he went."

"Well, dear, I suggest you get some sleep so you look refreshed in the morning for your breakfast. What will be will be, and the LWC is with you every step of the way as always."

"I certainly know that. What would I or any of us have done without each other?" Crawling into bed, Rita pulled the soft comforter up around her shoulders as Marge turned off the light. "Good night."

"Sweet dreams."

Soon Marge's rhythmic breathing echoed as she slept. But for Rita, sleep seemed to elude her. Her head and heart seemed to be in some sort of a struggle.

27

The sky was clear and the birds were serenading from nearby trees when the LWC got up to greet the day. They planned to meet in the lobby at seven, except Rita who would be preparing to meet up with Claude. The friends decided that since it was such a sunny morning in Seattle, they would head down the street to a neighborhood bakery and get some pastries and coffee then find a park to sit in.

At the park, Marge shared her conversation with Rita the night before. "What do you suppose is going to happen?" she asked.

"Well, breakfast should lend some clues, I hope," Marvel answered.

"Girls, I sure as heck hope our naïve friend is not about to get her heart broken. I just think he might be pulling the wool over her eyes," Kitty sighed.

"Well, he's wealthy in his own right and she certainly doesn't have riches, so it can't be that."

"We only have his word that he is wealthy," Kitty reminded them.

"All we need to remain being supportive no matter what. We can do that," Marvel argued.

*****

After doing some initial packing, Rita headed downstairs a few minutes before she was to meet her date. There waiting for her at the restaurant entrance was Claude bearing his striking smile, dressed casually in khakis and a polo shirt. As she approached him, she could see he was holding something behind his back. He greeted her warmly with a one-arm hug and kiss on the cheek. Rita, ever curious, asked, "What's behind your back?"

He produced a colorfully wrapped package tied up with a large yellow bow. Handing it to her, he suggested she wait to unwrap it once they sat down at their table. Rita loved getting gifts and was beaming as she carried it to the table in the back corner. Claude ordered them both a cup of coffee and a sweet roll to share. Leaving menus with them, their waitress went to fetch their coffee. Claude began looking over the menu. Rita tried to as well but she kept glancing at the package sitting next to her. Claude was peeking at her over his menu, chuckling to himself as he could see it was bugging her to no end not knowing what was in the gift. Finally, he thought he couldn't tease her anymore and asked her to open it.

Rita carefully removed the bow and ribbon and then took her time opening the taped ends so as not to tear the wrapping. Once removed, she folded it neatly into a square and placed near her purse. The box had a lid that was taped to keep it from popping open. Claude handed her his pocket knife to cut the tape with. Removing the lid, she looked inside. A big grin formed on her lips as she looked over at Claude and lifted the contents out of the box. It was a soft fuzzy teddy bear with a red ribbon around its neck. In its arms was an envelope with her name on it. As she opened it, she pulled out a card. Inside was a sweet poem that Claude had written for her. She didn't know what to say.

Claude reached across the table and took her hand. "Rita, I've so enjoyed your company. I hope you don't mind if we keep in touch. I would like to continue seeing you after this trip. Would that be all right?"

"Oh dear! Claude, I'm a little taken aback. I was hoping this was more than just a travel encounter, but I'm surprised you really want to continue seeing me."

"Surprised? What on earth for? You, Rita, are a gem. Your eyes sparkle like dancing stars, especially when you laugh, and your saccharine take on life is absolutely refreshing! Any man can see you are a rare woman indeed. I'd like to hope you see something in me too that you'd be willing to continue getting to know."

"Yes, I would like to remain in touch and see each other. I have no idea what my children will think though. Is this really happening to me? Oh my goodness!"

"The teddy bear is for you to think of me and hold close when we are apart," Claude revealed. Rita's eyes had filled with happy tears as Claude squeezed her hand. "Let's order some breakfast, shall we?"

Marge, Kitty, and Marvel entered the lobby just as Rita and Claude stepped out from the restaurant. Immediately, the girls noticed the teddy bear and that the couple was holding hands. Rita waved to her friends. They approached Rita and Claude as they hugged goodbye.

Claude gave her a tender kiss on the lips. "We'll talk soon." With that, he waved to the ladies and headed out to the street.

"Well?" they all asked at once.

Rita giggled and showed them the bear and the card he had given her. "We are going to stay in touch and try to see each another some more. He gave me the teddy bear to cuddle when I miss him. Isn't that sweet? Oh, and look, look! He wrote me a poem." She pointed out the poem to her friends. They all couldn't help but be happy for her.

Looking at her watch, Kitty declared it was time to finish packing and make their way to the station. Boarding the train, the friends drew stares and some smiles from fellow travelers, due to wearing the sweatshirts that Rita had made for them. They found seats on the upper level of the train, so they could watch the scenery as they left Seattle. The conductor told them that they would have a fantastic view of Mount Rainier today with the clear skies and sunshine. They didn't want to miss that for anything. They sat quietly as the train began to roll, each deep in her own thoughts.

Rita held the fuzzy bear in her lap, absentmindedly rubbing one of its soft ears as she gazed out the window. Had it really, only been a couple of weeks since they had begun this adventure? It seemed like yesterday, not a month ago! And Claude, she was so comfortable with him already. To think he wanted to continue seeing her! She never had imagined a romance might emerge on their trip, and certainly not a romance for her! She looked down at the bear and smiled demurely. He seemed to do and say all the right things. What did Kitty call that? She had said he was smooth. Yes, he was indeed, and she couldn't help being under his spell.

With the city's skyline minimizing, the passengers were directed to look out the south side of the train and get their cameras ready. There standing majestically in the morning sunlight was Mount Rainier, still wearing its top hat of snow. Outside of the clicking of cameras, the train car was quiet, reverence like, as everyone took in the glorious view. By early afternoon, Marvel and Marge felt the need to stretch their legs so they went off to visit the other cars. Kitty decided she needed a nap and left Rita sitting alone as she ambled back to the cabin.

With her friends gone, Rita pulled out Claude's card and reread the poem. The one thing Howie had never done for her was write a poem. It made her think about how different Howie and Claude were, which she decided was a good thing. She wouldn't want to be comparing the two men all the time and have Claude remind her of Howie. She wondered if Howie would be okay with her being interested in a new man. And Rita being Rita began to think about how she would feel if the situation was reversed. "Oh, for heaven's sake!" Rita chided herself. "I'd be gone and in glory. Of course I would want Howie to be happy." Now she felt better about her attraction to Claude, no more guilt that she was somehow cheating on her husband. With that, she smiled and took a long cleansing breath. It truly was time to move on with life!

Since there are not a lot of places to walk on a train, Marvel and Marge were back in no time. They had stopped by Marvel and Rita's cabin and picked up the pictures of their trip so far that she had developed in Seattle. The friends sorted through them and wrote on the backs of the pictures anything they wanted to remember. They came across the photos from the carriage ride to the inn in Sandpoint. Rita and Marvel teased Marge about the horse frightening her when the big mare wanted some treats from her pocket. Marge was a good sport and quickly pointed out that Bonnie and her teammate became her good buddies once they tasted her muffin. Rita had gotten a darling picture of Marge sharing her muffin with the two gentle giants.

"Marv, may I have this one?" asked Marge.

"We'll all make copies of all our pictures for one another," she responded. "But go ahead and take that one now. Seeing these photos make me miss Mollie, Ben, and Ida."

They all looked up as Kitty returned from her snooze. Marvel scooted over to the next seat so Kitty could join them. They filled her in on the conversation as they showed her the pictures.

"I'm so thankful for cameras, aren't you?" Kitty stated. "Ladies, we really had a nice journey, and it isn't through yet! I was thinking about what you just told me. The train stops in Sandpoint tomorrow anyway. We can find out how long the stopover is and perhaps see our friends for a bit. What d'ya say?"

"Wonderful! I know they will enjoy hearing about the rest of our vacation to Seattle."

"I'm excited to see them again!" Rita squealed.

They spent the entire day in the same seats with the expansive view, ordering snacks and sandwiches when they became hungry. It was such beautiful scenery they wanted to take in as much as possible before they were back in less picturesque landscape. The train continued to make its way through the mountains as the moon and stars made their entrance in the sky. Looking out the large window, Marvel pointed out the large luminous full moon.

Kitty reminded them, "Remember what Ida told us? The Native American population calls this particular moon, the Pink Moon. It's gorgeous!"

"Oh, look there, a shooting star!"

"Make a wish, ladies."

28

Back in Seattle, Stan and Gunnar shook hands, greeting with the man they knew as Quinton. They had dealt with him one other time and he had proven a useful source.

Quinton was the middleman for antique dealers in the Northwest region. He provided unique pieces to many shops and was well regarded as a top authenticator of antiques. What most didn't know was that he was a master at passing off replicas amongst the authentic pieces. He had been doing it a long time. What Quinton didn't realize was these two men standing here were using him to pass along high-class gems to their marks. He carefully touched and looked over each furniture piece Stan and Gunnar showed him. After reviewing the last one, he nodded and said one word, "Deal!"

Big smiles spread across the men's faces as they shook hands in agreement. A truck would be sent to pick up the furniture in the morning. At that time, money would be wired to an account Stan set up offshore. When they returned to Claude, they told him all went smoothly and that after tomorrow's transaction, they would close up shop and be on their way. Claude patted Gunnar on the back and gave Stan a thumbs-up.

*****

As the night gave way to dawn, Marvel awakened and was restless. She quietly exited the compartment she shared with Rita and walked toward the lounge car. Sitting at a corner table, she watched out the window. The sky was turning a light pink off in the distance. Within the next hour, the sky would look like a giant paint easel filled with pastel colors. She sighed with gratitude that she had often taken the time to observe and appreciate the Master's handiwork.

She found herself reminiscing about her life. As a young girl, she had preferred to be outdoors, often "camping out" in their back-yard with her sisters and friends. Her dad would build a bonfire. They would cook hotdogs on sticks and, naturally, would end the meal with roasted marshmallows and chocolate Hershey bar on a graham cracker, which was referred to as s'mores. As the fire turned to embers, she would stalk lightning bugs to catch and put in a jar so they could be tiny night lights in the tent. Her sisters never under-stood Marvel's fascination with bugs, lizards, and other creatures, but as long as she didn't make them handle any of it, they indulged her unique "pets." Her thoughts turned to her mom who shared her love of nature with Marvel. Together they had hunted pussy wil-lows, caught caterpillars, and watched them transform into cocoons and eventually emerge miraculously as butterflies. Her mother had shared in Marvel's delight when she would proudly bring in a toad or salamander even if her mom was entertaining neighbors for tea, as if that was the most normal thing for a little girl to do! After all these years, Marvel had to admit the ache she still felt over her mom's passing. What a tremendous life her mom had lived, and she was so thankful to have been her daughter.

The sky continued to brighten as the colors became vivid and spread over the horizon. Marvel checked her watch and decided to get a cup of coffee. Her short night would surely catch up with her at some point so she figured she had better get caffeine flowing in her system sooner rather than later. She headed to the dining car to sit and wait for her companions to join her. Not long after ordering her coffee, Marvel was joined by Marge and Rita.

"You were up and out early today, Marvel," Rita mentioned.

"Yeah, I woke up and couldn't go back to sleep. I felt restless and didn't want to disturb you so I went to watch the sunrise. It was magnificent!"

Marge knew her friend well. Not being able to go back to sleep was unusual for Marvel. She always was a sound sleeper. "So what is troubling you, dear?" she asked.

"I don't suppose anything, I just couldn't sleep."

"That is unlike you, and you know it!"

Marvel shrugged her shoulders and shook her head slightly, dismissing any more conversation about it.

When the waiter came to their table, he brought a pot of coffee and took their order. They all decided to eat a full breakfast so they could spend time today visiting with their friends in Sandpoint without concerning themselves with finding food. Rita asked the waiter what time they were scheduled to arrive in Sandpoint and was told they should be there by ten thirty a.m. Just as he turned to place their order, Kitty joined them. She told him quickly what she wanted and sat down. Holding out her mug, Marvel poured her a cup of coffee.

"So what have I missed?" asked Kitty.

"Not much. We'll arrive in Sandpoint by ten thirty according to our waiter. I'm excited to see our friends again," shared Marvel.

The friends chatted happily away as they ate and finished their coffee. The day promised to be partly sunny and mild. They were already a bit antsy and ready to get off the train and stretch their legs with a good walk.

29

The morning sun was glistening off the lake as the train pulled into Sandpoint Station. Wearing their walking shoes, the women excitedly departed their compartments, making sure to grab their sweatshirts and purses. Putting their sunglasses on as they stepped out of the station, they noticed Ida waving as she came closer.

"Hello, hello! So wonderful to see you again!" she called.

They all embraced and were talking at once. Laughing, they let each other go and began walking toward the parking lot. Ida brought the van to pick up some new guests staying for a few days. She offered her friends a lift back to the inn but they insisted on walking, declaring desperate need of exercise. Promising to catch up when they met back at the Magnolia, they set out walking through town. It had been a week since they were last here, but the scenery had already changed significantly. No more bare branches on the trees or bushes and the grass had turned green on most lawns. Gardens were being prepared for new seeds and flowers throughout the neighborhood. Snow and ice was now a distant memory.

As they walked up the front steps at the Magnolia Inn, Ida was already handing the room keys to the new guests. Mollie heard their voices as they entered and hurried out of the kitchen to welcome them. It had only been a week but she truly missed them. After the hugs, she showed them to the living room. Finding places to sit, they got comfy and began to tell Mollie and Ida about their time in Seattle. Of course, Mollie and Ida were especially interested in hearing about the romance budding between Rita and Claude. With a little encouragement, Rita opened up on their dinner and the teddy bear with the poem. Mollie and Ida gushed over the news. Rita turned slightly crimson. She had the poem in her purse and dug it out so they could read it. Reading it out aloud, Mollie looked around the room and winked at her friends. She made Rita promise to keep her up to date as she and Claude got to know one another better.

"Oh, I wish you brought the teddy bear," whined Ida. "I'll bet it is adorable!"

"It is," Rita assured her. "He has soft, fluffy, sort of a curly fur the color of nutmeg. He has big dark eyes, cute round ears, and is wearing a red satin ribbon. I admit I did cuddle him last night."

"What did you name him?"

"I haven't named him yet."

"How about Beau, since you got him from your beau and he is wearing a bow?"

"Aren't you clever? That is perfect!"

They were busy catching up on each other's week when Ben came through the front door carrying the mail.

"Looky here, Moll! We got a postcard from Seattle!" Turning the corner, he spied the ladies. He gave them a big grin and made sure to get a hug from each one of them. Ben nudged his wife to move over then he sat down in the big armchair she had curled up in. Putting his arm around her shoulders, he requested the ladies fill him in on their trip and asking to see any photos they had to share.

"Oh my goodness, the pictures! We have plenty to show you." Marge reached into her handbag and pulled out several pictures.

As they shared their memories of their adventures, Mollie and Ida were very intrigued with the photos of the arboretum and the variety of gardens. Mollie asked Marvel, "I don't see you in many of these garden pictures?"

"Oh, well, you see, I had a little accident."

"Accident?"

"Oh, here we go!" Marge sighed. "Let me tell you about *driving* luggage carts."

"Talking about *driving*, we have yet another story to share," added Marvel.

As they explained all about Marge running over Marvel's foot and the misdirection while driving home from the zoo, laughter filled the room. Tears were running down Mollie and Ida's faces.

Rita snorted, which always made them laugh harder. As they all held their sides, trying to catch their breath, they looked over at Marge who appeared to be laughing so hard it was silent. Then they heard it. Marge was *clucking* as she laughed. This set them all into fits of laughter again with the women crossing their legs tightly.

The day went far too quickly. It was time to head back to the train station. Mollie delivered a care package of fresh baked goodies to Kitty for their trip. Ben went out to pull the van around to give the ladies a lift to the train station. Once again, they hugged and promised to stay in touch. With that, the LWC climbed into the van and turned to wave good-by as Ben backed out of the driveway.

30

After a short nap, the LWC met up in the lounge car. Kitty brought the cookies Mollie had baked for them. They all ordered tea. Marge and Rita pulled out the photos to look over again.

"We sure got some nice pictures, didn't we?" Marvel smiled.

"We had so much fun! What fantastic memories we will have for the rest of our lives!" added Marge.

As they talked amongst themselves, a couple approached them. Looking up, they realized it was Terry and Roxanne.

"Please join us! We didn't see you on the train when we left Seattle," offered Kitty.

"Oh well, actually, Terry had some side business stops he needed to make so we drove here. I'm so happy that you are on the train now too. We can compare notes on our time in Seattle," gushed Roxanne.

So they spent the next hour sharing pictures and swapping stories. Slyly, Roxanne turned the conversation to Claude and Gunnar. She wanted to hear all about their time with the attractive brothers. As the conversation broadened, Terry asked the ladies if the men made any inquiries about their pensions and investments. Kitty and Marvel's eyebrows rose as they looked around at one another. Rita, not thinking anything of the questions, babbled on about telling them all about Howie's preparation for her after he was gone. Marvel admitted that she too had shared similar information with the gentlemen.

"They were just making conversation," said Rita. "They were genuinely concerned that we remain comfortable in this final chapter of our lives."

"They were willing to advise us with investing if we had questions. However, they told both of us that it seems our husbands had done a quality job providing for us," Marvel added. Terry seemed to be mulling this over. Kitty had to wonder why he seemed so interested.

*****

The day was slipping into dusk as the train carried them closer to home. The LWC moved up to the upper level to watch the sun and moon exchange places overhead. It was too early for any of them to want to turn in for the evening so they sauntered into the lounge car and found a table. On the way, Marge stopped by the cabinet with games and cards and found what she was looking for. She sat down with her friends and put the game of Yahtzee on the table in front of them. Pulling out her pen, she announced that she'd keep score.

Grabbing the cup and the dice, Marvel decided to go first. "Ya know, playing games like this makes me miss raising our family. We'd always be together for supper and afterward, before homework or TV, we'd play a game or two of something. It was fun and connected us with our children. Whether they meant to or not, they always shared things about themselves, friends, or school that we might not have heard otherwise."

"I think that is a key ingredient that families of this generation are missing, don't you?" added Kitty.

"Some of our most fun memories were the laughter and shenanigans we shared while playing games as a family. That was what my husband referred to as 'our secret to raising good kids' as he put it. It leveled the playing field between parents and children so they could just enjoy being together."

Marge conspiratorially admitted they used games to help with their children's education, like keeping score to work on math. "And now I witness my children doing the same for my grandchildren."

When it came back around to Marvel, she rolled three fives and two threes. "Full house!" she claimed. "My Al had very specific ways of playing Yahtzee and how he chose to put what score in which category. For instance, he really didn't like getting a Yahtzee with bigger numbers. The sixes or fives, he claimed was a waste of high points to be played elsewhere. We always told him he didn't have to claim those Yahtzee's but he would grudgingly take it anyway. He was so funny that way!"

They continued to take turns as the scorecard filled up. Kitty had taken it upon herself to suggest what score her friends should put where, claiming that she had a method.

31

Traveling by Greyhound bus wasn't as expensive as the train or as fast as a plane, but they could travel without revealing what was in their bags and get recognized. The three men split up in Montana. Stan rented a car while the brothers continued their travel via bus. The seating was comfortable enough for them to nap off and on. They only got off at stops to stretch their legs and grab a bite to eat. They were on a mission to get back home before their merchandize arrived.

As Gunnar dozed, Claude looked at some pictures they had from their trip. He lingered on several that had Rita. He found himself tracing her facial features with his finger and realized he missed her. That naïve, cheerful sprite of a lady had gotten to him. He shook his head absentmindedly. Never would he have suspected having such feelings for someone again, especially someone like her. Their plan had worked so many times before. He and Gunnar had very successfully seduced unsuspecting widows out of money before, but this time he couldn't do it. It had been part of the initial plan, but circumstances had changed his course of action. Of course, he now recognized that business had been complicated by his feelings. She definitely caught his heart off guard. Well, when they were back home, he would call her up and take her out that very week. He needed to see her again.

*****

It was only hours now before they were home, the LWC was growing restless. They had been gone a long time, which now felt like a year. They were all excited to see their children and grandchildren and share their journey with them. They missed their pets and their homes. It had been a very special—needed even—time away, but all were ready to come *home*.

Kitty found a new novel to keep her from watching the clock. Rita had begun a new project. Marge and Marvel sat upstairs, watching the landscape go by as it slowly changed from sparse country to lakes and trees.

Marge looked over at her lifelong friend and studied her. "Marv, what's on your mind?"

"What? Oh goodness, Marge! Not a whole lot. Why?"

"Because I know you. You seemed to embrace this trip at first, really enjoy it, but somewhere, something changed."

"Oh you! I guess you think you know me pretty well, huh? Yes, I think a vital realization hit me while we were on our journey. I should thank you."

"Thank me? Whatever for?"

"Because you do know me, maybe better than I know myself! Don't think I don't know that this trip was brought about because my bestest buddy knew I needed to stop feeling sorry for myself and start living life again!"

"I have no idea—"

"Stop! Yes, you do. Thank you, and I love you!"

"Okay, what have you figured out?"

"Time to find out what I'm still on this planet for. My identity is beyond Al's wife and being a mom or grandma. Those are just perks!" Marvel reached over and embraced her friend's hand. Smiling with tears in her eyes, she added, "I don't know what it all is going to be yet, but I sure as heck want you by my side when I figure it out. Okay?"

"You got it!"

32

The sun was out with wispy clouds floating through the sky as the train arrived into the Twin Cities. The LWC were all packed and ready to greet the spring air in Minnesota. They could feel the train begin to slow as it neared the station. Watching the city skyline as they approached, it appeared in a fresh way. They had seen so much beauty throughout their travel, but there was something beautifully sacred about returning home. Once the train stopped, they gathered their bags and got off.

At the station, some of their children greeted them when they got off the train. It was wonderful to see and hold them. Their grandchildren must have grown three inches since they left! Hugs and kisses all around. Marvel's daughter offered to take a picture of the LWC together at the end of their journey. Gathering in front of the train, the women squeezed in together. They had grown as individuals and as friends through this vacation and couldn't be happier that they had done it. As the families heard bits and pieces while they gathered all the bags, Kitty noticed Terry and Roxanne approaching them. The women introduce them to their families.

Roxanne was friendly and greeted them all, but Terry seemed preoccupied. Finally, he turned to Rita and asked, "Did Claude ever give you anything?"

"What? Why are you asking me that?"

"Mom, who is this guy?" asked Rita's daughter.

"Rita, again, did Claude or Gunnar ever give you or any of you anything to carry for them?"

"Heavens no!" Rita blurted out.

"Ah, Rita, Beau," reminded Marvel.

"What? You can't be talking about a teddy bear!"

"Teddy bear?" asked her daughter.

Now Rita was flustered. This isn't how she wanted to tell her family about Claude. "I met a nice man. He gave me a teddy bear on our last day together. That's all."

Terry asked, "May I see this teddy bear please?"

Rita looked helplessly at her friends and then over to Roxanne who nodded to her. Reaching in her carry-on bag she pulled out the teddy bear that become known as Beau. She handed him to Terry who gently took it from her hands.

He ran his fingers over the bear and looked closely at the stitching in his arms and legs. He handed the bear to Roxanne. She too looked over it carefully and then removed the satin ribbon. Studying the neck seam, she glanced over at Terry. She pointed out a few stitches that did not resemble the original stitches. "Rita, please indulge me. I need to pull these few stitches out. I'll sew him back up."

"Go ahead, I can sew him back up."

"Wait, what are you looking for?" Kitty demanded.

Without answering, Roxanne skillfully removed the stitches and turned the bear upside down. Feeling around in the opening, she pulled out several stones of rubies, sapphires, and diamonds. The women were speechless!

Finally, Rita's daughter commented, "What the heck is going on? Are you accusing my mom of smuggling? Do you know how absolutely ridiculous that is??"

Terry spoke up. "We've been following a smuggling ring for several years now. It has taken us many hours to put the pieces together. I don't believe your mother smuggled these but I do believe she was used."

Her friends and family turned to Rita who looked horrified and heartbroken. Tears formed her eyes, but she wasn't sure if they were from sadness, betrayal, or anger.

"And you?" Marge asked Roxanne.

"Terry is my partner. We are with the FBI. I'm sorry to have misled you. We were doing our job."

"So what next?" asked Kitty.

"We'll see if Rita or any of you are contacted by the men. We'll have a plan in place."

"So this whole thing was a setup? None of it was true?" Rita whispered. Her friends hugged her close.

"No, Rita, I don't buy that. Claude cared for you. All you had to do was look at him looking at you," Marvel told her.

Terry and Roxanne looked at one another. "Actually, I do believe he really cares for you, Rita. He didn't scam you and your friends out of money like he has others. I think the circumstances made them change their game plan and decided to at least get something out of it all, smuggling the gems through an unsuspecting friend. I actually believe he will be in touch with you soon so we'll coach you on how to proceed."

Terry and Roxanne gave the ladies and families the okay to head home and that they would be in touch the following day.

Sliding into their cars the friends with their families departed. This wasn't the ending the LWC anticipated of their first adventure together, but it certainly turned out to be more adventurous than any of them could have dreamed of.

33

Back in her own bed with the two cats and dog snuggled next to her, Marvel thought about the day. No one had seen that ending coming! She reached over and grabbed her phone, dialing Rita. On the third ring, Rita answered.

"Hi, Marv! Miss me already?"

"Hi, sweetie! Just wondering how you are doing. Today had a tough ending."

"I'll be okay. It's good to be home, to real life."

"Rita, our trip was *real life* too. I don't think for one second that Claude's feelings toward you were imaginary. He cares about you, I could tell. I'm good at telling those things."

"Marv, you are a dear. I'll be all right. I'm a little hurt and embarrassed, of course. My daughter Lisa stayed with me tonight. We had a good girl talk. I'll admit it was fun to have a man's attention again, but I had Howie, and that is good enough for me."

Marvel was struck by her friend's composure and strength and said a quick prayer, thanking God that Rita's daughter was so supportive. "Rita, you and I might be learning similar things about ourselves in different ways, but I believe we are on the same path. Let's talk soon. I'm only a phone call away if you need someone to talk to. Love you."

"Love you too. Good night."

The next morning while Rita was drinking her coffee, she made breakfast for herself and her daughter. The phone rang. Picking it up, she heard the baritone voice she had come to know and long for. "Why, Claude, is that you?" she cooed.

"Hi, Rita. I have been thinking about you, about us. I miss you."

"I've been thinking about you too, Claude. I named my teddy bear Beau."

"Oh, I like it! Is he keeping you in good company?"

"Not at the moment, but all the way home I cuddled him."

"Rita, when can I see you?"

"Oh my! You caught me off guard. I am delighted you called, but I guess I didn't think you really would."

"Why wouldn't I? I told you I would." Just then, Rita's daughter strolled into the kitchen. She caught the look on her mom's face and knew it was the man who had given her the bear. She nodded positively. That was the support she needed so she told Claude that they could meet up that very weekend. "Rita, you seem tense. Did I call at a bad time?"

"Actually, yes. My daughter is with me. Missed her ol' mom, I guess."

"All right. May I call you later?"

"Absolutely!"

After they hung up, her daughter hugged her mom tightly. "It's going to be all right, Mom." Rita's eyes stung with tears once more as she contemplated her feelings for Claude and that it had all been a bad fairy tale. She wondered what Howie would think of her foolishness. As if her daughter read her thoughts, she said, "Ya know, Mom, Daddy would say,"—she lowered her voice—"'Rita, honey, that big ol' heart of yours is too trusting, but please don't ever change!' I can just hear him now."

*****

Marvel woke up that morning thinking about Claude and the others. They sure had her fooled. They had been such gentlemen and seemed so genuine. Kitty's suspicions had been correct all along! She was thankful that Kitty was so supportive when they learned the news yesterday. She was usually suspicious of everyone until she got to know them, but she put her arm around her friend and said softly, "I guess I'm rather protective of those I choose as friends." That brought a little smile to Rita's lips.

34

Humming to herself, Marvel began to unpack, setting aside the dirty clothing for laundry. Her cat, Dickens, sniffed around and decided to get inside the suitcase. Following his lead, the other cat, Moxie, joined him. Soon the two were curled up amongst her remaining clothes, purring loudly and giving her loving looks. Since she had come home, her pets hadn't allowed her any space. She had to be sure to be careful if taking a backwards step so she didn't step on the dog.

Marge felt restless as she found herself scurrying around from room to room in her house. She felt like she had so much to do, she couldn't focus on just one project. She knew she had to go grocery shopping today because she found her refrigerator and pantry quite bare. Luckily, her milk hadn't gone bad and she still had a half box of cereal so at least she could have breakfast. Looking around her cozy home, she realized she was missing her traveling companions. The trip had been both trying at times, but very bonding too. She decided to check in on them. First, she decided to call Marvel. Their conversation quickly turned to Claude and Gunnar. "My heavens, Marv! How could we have been so daft?"

"They are very good at what they do and were even more convincing since I believe Claude's feelings for Rita were real. What do we know about flimflam anyway? I want to believe people are basically honest."

"How do you suppose our girl is feeling? Maybe we should go and see her to cheer her up?"

"I have an idea, Marge. Let's get our pictures together, buy some albums or scrapbooks, and bring them to her to start putting together. We can let Kitty know what we are up to. She can join us if she isn't too busy."

They agreed to meet to get what they would need and hung up.

*****

Lisa answered the door when she heard knocking. She found her mom's pals loaded down with shopping bags. Peeking above the bags, Marvel greeted her and walked in with Marge at her heels.

Rita came from the kitchen as they were setting their bags on the dining room table. "What have we got here?"

"We decided you needed a distraction and a project!" Marge announced. The women embraced then unloaded the sacks of photos, albums, and supplies.

Lisa remarked, "Well, it looks as though you ladies are set. Mom, I'm going to pick you up some groceries and drop off your dry cleaning. Have fun!"

Rita blew her daughter a kiss and sat down at the table to decide how they wanted to proceed. They had been separating photos, postcards, and other paper souvenirs they collected for about forty minutes when the doorbell rang. "It's open!" Rita called out.

In came Kitty. She too brought photos from their trip. It felt good to be together again. This project was the perfect back cover of their adventure. None of them mentioned Claude and Gunnar. They just wanted to be together and reminisce.

Finally, Rita spoke up. "Claude called me this morning." Silence fell over the room as her friends looked over at her. "I told him I couldn't really talk since Lisa was with me and we were making breakfast. He asked if he could call me later and I told me yes."

"So how are you doing? What are you going to say?" Kitty ventured.

"Well, I have a call into Terry and Roxanne. I'm waiting to hear from them. I have to admit it was nice to hear his voice, but I have such jumbled emotions. I just don't know what to think or feel!"

"Rita, that's very understandable," reasoned Marvel. "Let's just wait to see what Terry wants you to say or do to begin with. Ah, honey, we all believe he does really care for you. It's just too bad he chose what he chose. That doesn't make your feelings any less real just because he is a con artist. I think he let you see a lot of his true self. For that, you can feel thankful."

"Oh, I know, I know. How can attraction do that to us so fast? Turned me right back into a school girl with a crush on the popular boy. So silly!"

"That is why we can't rely solely on feelings, they can be misleading. But, may I add, misleading or not, they are a powerful influence."

"It goes to show us that we may be *old*, but we sure *ain't* dead!" laughed Marvel. "Actually, it makes me happy to know love is love no matter what stage of life one is in. I find an odd comfort in that!"

*****

The afternoon sailed by as they worked on their project. Lisa came back with groceries and made them all a tasty lunch. Terry called back and coached Rita on how to proceed with Claude. By four thirty, they were packing up for the day. Hugging at the door, they all gave Rita advice and told her they'd be praying and waiting to hear from her.

As she closed the door, she was overcome with gratitude for such supportive friends. "Lisa, I hope you have friends in your life like the ones I have in mine. I just don't know what I'd do without 'em!"

The phone rang, it was Claude. Rita sat down in the comfy armchair in her living room. Her daughter, hearing the start of the conversation, brought her mom a small glass of wine, kissed the top of her head, and waved goodbye. Claude and Rita talked easily, catching up on the remainder of their travels; Rita taking care to leave some specific events out of the conversation. Terry had coached her well and had given her confidence on this next important step. Claude felt relieved that Rita seemed more like the woman he had gotten to know over the past few weeks. He had been a little unsettled after their earlier phone call that day. They agreed to meet up the following evening for dinner. Claude offered to pick her up but upon Terry's instructions, she told him she'd meet him at the restaurant.

As they hung up, Rita had such mixed emotions. She was nervous about the encounter but excited to see Claude again. She walked into her bedroom and lifted Beau into her arms. She hugged him gently then traced his darling face with her fingertips, wishing that little bear had never appeared. Setting him down again in her rocking chair, she looked at herself in the mirror. She saw a gullible little old lady looking back at her. Until yesterday, she had seen a different reflection, a woman of experienced vitality and a lot left to live for. Now she didn't know who that woman was.

35

The ever faithful Last Wives' Club would never allow one of their own to face a daunting challenge alone. It had been decided that they would meet prior to Rita's dinner with Claude. They encouraged their friend and left to find seats in a booth in the back of the restaurant so as not to be seen by Claude.

Thirty minutes passed, Rita walked into the restaurant to meet Claude. He was there waiting for her. He greeted her with a strong hug and a kiss on the cheek. Rita couldn't help but blush at his affection. It was good to see him.

"Don't you look lovely!" he praised.

"You are sweet," she answered demurely. "And look at your handsome self! It's nice to see you again, Claude."

Their table was ready. Her friends made it clear to the hostess where to seat them so she showed the couple to a cozy table near the gas fireplace. Even though it was spring and the weather was warming up, the glow of the fire added a homey feeling. As they looked over the menu, Claude glanced at Rita and smiled. She had the same look of unable to make up her mind as he remembered. He touched her hand, which made her jump a bit. His eyebrows arched upward and commented about her jumpiness.

"Oh, sorry! Just deep in thought trying to decide what I'm hungry for."

"I figured. That's why I was going to suggest something, if I may."

"Oh, please do!"

He told her of a couple of things that were specialties of the house and what he would order. By the time the waitress came, they had made up their minds to share one of the large steaks and Rita ordered an extra salad. Through the course of dinner, Rita asked about the furniture shipment and how it all went. He was pleased to report all the pieces were in good shape and had gone on to be sold at various venues. She asked him how he had gotten into the importing business so he gave her a little of his background with his father's tutelage who raised him and Gunnar to be businessmen. He shared how he would get restless and bored though with the same old same old so after meeting others through business transactions, he found himself in the import-export business, much like Stan. It was always different. New clients, new places, and new wares so it was stimulating to him. He proved successful in the industry so that is where he landed, bringing Gunnar along after some cajoling.

"That's enough about my business. Why the sudden interest?"

"Well, I thought we were trying to get to know one another better. I want to know what makes you tick. Besides, my daughter had all sorts of questions!" Rita smiled at him.

"Ah, the protective cub, eh? Fair enough. I'm sure my children will have some questions about you too."

Rita's phone buzzed that she had a text message. She excused herself to go to the restroom. Waiting for her in the restroom were the rest of her posse. They had heard from Roxanne. They were ready and waiting for Rita to spring the trap. Returning to the table, Claude rose to pull out her chair for her to sit. Rita now found his gentleman politeness off-putting because she saw it all as a show to disarm her. She smiled and thanked him then decided to get right to it.

"Claude, may I ask you something?"

"Of course. Anything."

"Well, you know how I enjoy doing crafts, knitting, sewing, and things like that." He nodded his agreement. "Well, I noticed a slight tear in Beau, the teddy bear you gave me, and I went to sew it up." Rita watched Claude carefully. *Oh, he is good!* He just continued to look into her eyes and listen actively. She pressed on. "I noticed something hard in the neck so I stuck my finger in the hole to see what it was before I fixed the tear. And I found this." Holding out her hand, she showed him a beautiful sapphire stone. He didn't say anything but picked up the stone from her hands and studied it. "How do you suppose that got in there?" she asked him. Looking up at her, she could see in his eyes a hint of hardness and perhaps a little sadness.

"I wouldn't know. Anything else?"

"How could you not know? Are you saying that when you bought me the bear, it already had gems hidden in it?"

Claude looked at Rita and sighed. "Okay, I'll tell you the truth. I guess you deserve that from me. Stan is not who he claims to be. Oh, he is in importing all right—importing stolen gems! Gunnar and I met him a while ago. He got stuck in a hard place so we told him we would help him this one time." Rita looked at him skeptically. "Rita, my feelings for you are genuine. I adore you. I was just trying to help out a friend who found himself in a jam. I'm sorry I ended up putting you in the mix."

She couldn't believe what she was hearing. Terry and Roxanne had told her that they had been tracking this ring of thieves for quite some time. So now he was lying to her face. She turned her eyes from him, not wanting to let him see her eyes filling with tears.

"Rita, say something please!" Claude pleaded. Before she could respond, Terry and Roxanne approached their table. He looked up and smiled a slow smile. "Now I know who you are," he said to them. "I believe I've been set up!"

"No!" Rita replied, angry and hurt. "I was the one set up. Claude, how could you?"

Claude looked over at her and reached for her hands. She pulled them quickly away. He looked wounded, but she didn't care at that moment. It was all she could do not to cry. Terry took Claude's arm so he would stand up. Turning him around, he handcuffed him and led him out. Roxanne sat down with Rita and told her she did the right thing. Reaching in her purse, she pulled out the recording device and handed it to Roxanne. Roxanne got up, paid the dinner tab, and left. Suddenly, Rita was surrounded by her friends.

"Let's get out of here and go someplace to talk," suggested Kitty.

Scooping up their hurt friend, the LWC departed.

36

They decided to head to Rita's house. Once there, Kitty put some water on for tea and hot cocoa. Marge found some cookies in the pantry and placed them on a plate for the friends to share. Marvel sat by Rita on the couch and had her arm around her, letting her cry. Tears were cleansing and Marvel encouraged her to let it all out. After a few minutes, the tears subsided and Rita's breathing returned to normal. Kitty brought in the tea and cocoa and sat down in the armchair across from the love seat where Marge sat. Then they waited for Rita to speak. They were not going to hurry her as she processed what occurred. In fact, they were all still processing the events of the evening.

Finally, Rita spoke, softly at first. "Girls, I feel so foolish! I can't imagine what you all must think of me!"

Kitty spoke up. "Think of you? Why, you are one of the strongest people I've ever met and courageous! That took a lot gumption to do what you did tonight. I'm proud to call you my friend!" The others nodded in agreement.

"We are just sorry that your heart was broken because of the whole thing!" Marge conveyed.

"He was so attentive, fun, and, dare I admit it, dashing!"

"Rita, we all agree with you. He and Gunnar were all of those things and more. On top of it all, we were all a little lonely for male companionship. I don't know about you all, but I felt somewhat like a coed again, and I liked it!" said Marge. Again, they all nodded in agreement.

Marvel, the ever present optimist, added, "Rita, it was so fun to see a special glint in your eyes, and I have to say it was fun to be a little flirtatious again. I am thankful for it all even though it ended the way it did. But on the bright side, we helped nail some folks the law has been after for quite some time. Feels pretty good when you look at it that way, doesn't it?"

The friends talked into the night. Marvel didn't want Rita to be alone so she had her pack an overnight bag, put food out for her cat, and brought her to her house. Getting Rita tucked into her guest room, Marvel left and closed the door.

Soon Rita heard something bumping the door so she went to check it out. In came Moxie with a loud meow and jumped up on the bed. Rita chuckled and welcomed the cat. As she crawled under the covers, Moxie patiently waited for Rita to get situated and then promptly curled up on her legs, purring loudly. Rita smiled. *We are never left all alone*, she thought. *I have a lot to be thankful for.* Then she closed her eyes for a sound night's sleep.

Topping the headlines in the local section of the paper the next morning was the story of Claude's arrest. They had located one of the partners, and he too had been apprehended. The article explained that Claude and others had been importing stolen gems from around the world for many years as well as scamming people through various plots, never staying long in one location and traveling by way of car, train, and bus to avoid inspection of their luggage. They deceived people out of hundreds of thousands of dollars by passing fake antique pieces and paintings off as authentic. The article went on about the law finally getting the break they needed by some unsuspecting citizens and those same citizens helped led to the arrest. No names were given out, but there was a photograph of Claude being handcuffed and Rita sitting at the table.

"Oh my goodness!" exclaimed Rita when she saw it. "I don't want my face all over regarding this!"

"I think it's too late. You might want to call your children and let them know what went on."

"Lisa knows part of the story so I just have to fill her in. However, her brother might have a fit especially if he gets wind of this before I have a chance to tell him. I'll just go in the other room and call him."

Marvel's landline rang. It was Marge who had also seen the paper.

*****

Several weeks went by, and the LWC all went back into normal life. Terry and Roxanne had been keeping them up to date on the investigation and discovery of the many things these men had been involved with. Stan had been found and arrested as well. Claude and Gunnar pled guilty to lesser charges and helped the feds locate Stan so at least the ladies wouldn't have to be witnesses in a trial.

It was almost Memorial Day weekend and they all were going to be spending it with some family members. Summer was around the corner and everyone seemed in good spirits. The friends made sure to get together at least once or twice a month. Tonight they met at one of their favorite places. They were getting caught up in all their children's and grandchildren's lives as they shared a meal. Marvel told them how she had recently received a letter from Mollie back in Sandpoint, asking how they were all doing after the realization they had been romanced by criminals. The ladies laughed as they recounted the phone call they all made together to tell Mollie and Ida what had happened.

Marge picked up her wine glass and tapped it with her knife. "Ladies, a toast! To the Last Wives' Club and our adventures. Looking forward to what lies ahead!" They all clinked glasses.

"Marge, you said *adventures*. We've only been on one," Marvel teased.

"Oh, but wait." Reaching into her purse, Marge pulled out various pamphlets, passing them around. "Where should we head off to next?"

Kitty, who had just taken a sip of wine, coughed and spit it all over.

Acknowledgements

A special thank you to Johanna Harmon, John Townsend, Janine Weatherby, Carole Peter, Rebecca Meade and Connie Peterson!

About the Author

Joan was born and raised in a suburb of Saint Paul, Minnesota. She loves the four seasons, winters and all! She is the youngest of six children. Her passion has long been animals, horses being her favorite.

Joan studied sociology and anthropology at Gustavus Adolphus College in Saint Peter, Minnesota. After college, she attempted working the normal nine-to-five but was easily bored with routine days. That's when her career path took an unusual turn. She took a job as an assistant trainer for a friend who had opened her own stable. Over the years, she moved on to other horse training opportunities, traveling and showing horses in many different states. Due to unplanned circumstances, she and her daughter moved in with her parents. One of those unexpected circumstances was the diagnosis of her dad with Alzheimer's disease.

When dealing with a family member who has an incurable illness, our perceptions often change. Watching her loving dad slowly lose his memory and the things he cherished was heart-wrenching. Joan's mom went to the nursing home every day, long after he had no idea who she was. Joan watched the friendships evolve of her mom and other wives whose husbands were in the nursing home. This eventually inspired her first book.

Joan's stories revolve around the inevitable trials life throws our way, challenges that many of us face day to day. The characters are engaging and easy to relate to as they face unforeseen twists of fate.

CPSIA information can be obtained
at www.ICGtesting.com
Printed in the USA
FSHW011549221218
54415FS